Two by Each

Mystery Novel Circa 1950
New Bedford, MA

By

Clement R. Beaulieu

Two by Each

Mystery Novel Circa 1950 New Bedford, MA

By

Clement R. Beaulieu

Visit our website **at www.StillwaterPress.com** for more information.

First Stillwater River Publications Edition

ISBN-10: 0-692-56700-3
ISBN-13: 978-069256700-5

1 2 3 4 5 6 7 8 9 10
Written by Clement R. Beaulieu
Back Cover Art by Julia Beaulieu
Cover design by Dawn M. Porter.
Published by Stillwater River Publications, Glocester, RI, USA.

Two by Each

To

Joyce

This mystery is a work of fiction. It follows my two prior mystery novels, **Bad Lucky Number** circa 1930 and **Round Corners** circa 1940. It continues to focus on persons from New Bedford, MA. Some of the historical personages mentioned in connection with the events of the story actually existed. The time of this story, **TWO by EACH**, is circa 1950.

The main characters of the story are fictional. The waterfront and historic sections of New Bedford are the setting of many events. Various individuals have shared actual events and circumstances that help to put a touch of realism to this tale. However, any resemblance to actual persons living or dead is strictly coincidental.

A special thanks to Michael DeConinck who provided the photograph of his fishing boat, the **Millpoint** that was used for the front cover of the book. My daughter, Julia, has again provided an original watercolor that is used as the background of the back cover. I am grateful to my niece, Joyce, who started me on the path of writing novels and enthusiastically continues to support my efforts. Special consideration goes to Lee Bordas, one of my readers and critics. I am grateful for the support that my wife Jo-Ann brings to these projects.

Two by Each

Book One

Two by Each
Book One
Chapter One

November 1950's

Claude Lepage greeted Raphael as he entered the rear door of the Paradise Luncheonette. It was 4:30 on a Monday morning.

"How was your weekend?" inquired Claude.

"Your brother Al and our families gathered for Sunday dinner at my folks' house. My two daughters, Rachel and Claire, who are close to being very sophisticated teenagers, let their hair down as they played with their younger cousins. They went down to the pond, took their shoes off and ran along the sandy beach. They screamed as they put their feet into the water that is getting colder after these frosty mornings this past week," Raphael replied.

Raphael put on his apron and started to prepare the batter for his fluffy pancakes. Claude was just taking the last of his rolls out of the baking ovens.

"I was planning to make cranberry muffins, this morning," stated Claude. "What other types of muffins do you think I should make?"

"Since you add a bit of corn meal to your cranberry muffin batter, I would skip that one. The bran muffins are popular on a Monday. They seem to act like a laxative after the heavy eating on the weekend. I would also make a small batch of chocolate chip muffins. They're not my favorite. They're too much like a dessert, but they are growing in popularity with some of our customers."

Both worked quietly and quickly at their separate work areas of the kitchen. As he placed the muffin baking pans into the ovens, Claude turned to Raphael who was placing long strips of bacon on the griddle getting them partially cooked and draining the greasy fat, so that he could later quickly prepare an order of bacon with eggs or pancakes. The aroma was moving through the kitchen and Claude raised his voice in order for Raphael to hear him over the sizzling bacon on the griddle.

"I was planning to leave by 6:30," said Claude. "My wife, Anne, had a miscarriage this past Thursday. She was less than three months pregnant. We were all disappointed. This was a great setback for Anne who has been gradually getting over her shyness and nervousness."

"I'm so sorry," said Raphael as he placed a spatula under a dozen slices of partially cooked bacon on the griddle and placed them on a baking sheet.

"I was planning to get home early enough to walk with her to her classroom at Normandin Junior High. She is anxious about meeting her fellow teachers who knew of her pregnancy and had been so happy for her. She had considered missing school this morning but I think I convinced her last night that it would be best to face her fears sooner than later." Claude continued.

"Once you have the muffins out of the oven, get on your way," encouraged Raphael. "The waitress will be in shortly to make the coffee and set up the counter and tables for breakfast. Once the muffins are cooled she'll place them on the counter where the aroma will make them irresistible."

Claude's white pants and shirt were still covered by a layer of flour as he exited the back door of the luncheonette. He waved to Raphael who was paying close attention to his griddle. It took concentration to just partially cook the bacon and drain off the hot grease without getting burned.

Claude jumped on the first bus going north. At this time of day the busses on Acushnet Avenue went by every fifteen minutes. He got off at the Baylies Square bus stop. He quickly walked down the street to the apartment that he and Anne shared with her parents just across the street from his family's home. He was hoping and praying that Anne was up and getting herself ready for her day at school. After their discussion the previous evening, Anne had started to prepare her class material. Anne taught English literature to seventh and eighth graders. Claude, who didn't spend much time reading, had found that Anne's latest book that her class was reading, *A Tale of Two Cities*, was very interesting if not exciting.

Claude tried to be quiet climbing the front stairs so as not to disturb the elderly woman who lived in the apartment below the Saulniers in this six family house. There was a very different atmosphere in the three-decker across the street where all the apartments were filled with Lepages with large families and youngsters who made themselves welcomed at any doorway.

As he unlocked and opened the door to the apartment, Claude was relieved to see that light was escaping from under the door of their bedroom. He opened the door quietly hoping not to disturb Anne's parents who usually didn't get up until 9. Mr. Saulnier worked the second shift at the Acushnet Company plant just down the street.

Anne was dressed in a bright-colored dress and was a vision of beauty in Claude's eyes. He quickly went over to grab her but she held him off. She pointed to the baking flour that still covered him. In his enthusiasm at seeing Anne ready for her day, he had forgotten. Claude went to the front hall and hung up his whites used at the restaurant. After a quick wash, he returned to their bedroom and found that Anne had placed his black pants, white shirt and black tie on the bed. He changed quickly and put on black shoes that he had polished over the weekend. After accompanying Anne to her school, he would be off to his second job as a chauffeur.

Before leaving the apartment, Anne peeked into her parent's room and saw that her mother had her eyes open. Anne went up to her to kiss her. Mrs. Saulnier sat up and hugged her precious daughter.

"I will pray that you will have a good day, Anne," encouraged her mother. "You are a strong and brave woman."

Anne and Claude walked up the street to catch the bus to Lund's Corner. Claude now had a black cap and coat. It was quite a contrast from his early morning attire. Anne had a warm long grey coat over her dress and a pale green kerchief held her long, carefully combed hair in place as they walked along. The weather had turned damp, no longer the colder, crisp days they had experienced over the weekend. Claude carried her large bag of school material and hand in hand they arrived at the school by 7:00. Anne kissed Claude on the sidewalk as other teachers were arriving for another school day.

She whispered in his ear, "Thank you for walking with me to school this morning."

Two by Each

Chapter Two

After watching Anne enter the school building in the company of the other teachers, Claude walked quickly up the street to Ashley Boulevard. There he took the bus to the center of New Bedford. He welcomed the warmth of the bus. It was turning out to be one of those damp, cold days that could chill one to the bone.

Upon exiting the bus, he walked a few blocks to a six space garage. He lifted the piece of black rubber that covered the pad lock of the garage door. After opening the two doors of the garage space and placing a stone to hold one door that was being blown shut by the wind coming off the waters of Buzzards Bay, Claude backed up a shiny black Lincoln Cosmopolitan.

He was running on a very tight schedule so he didn't wipe down the auto that had sat in the garage over the weekend. He proceeded to the home of his employer, former Lieutenant Mortimer Spooner Weigand, on Mechanics Lane. He was behind in his schedule by about ten minutes but he gauged that he still had sufficient time to bring Mr. Weigand to his eight o'clock meeting at the Whaling City National Bank.

As he approached the residence, he saw Mrs. Moriarity pacing up and down the small veranda. When she saw the car approaching, she rushed down the three steps to the sidewalk.

"What's the matter, Mrs. Moriarity?" Claude inquired as he approached her after parking the car.

"Master Mortimer is not home. He was not in the house when I arrived to make his breakfast and there is no sign that he slept here last night," answered Mrs. Moriarity as she nervously twisted her hands. "His well-worn brief case is still at the side of his desk in the front room and his bed is as I left it on Sunday morning," she continued.

Claude knew that this was not typical behavior for his employer who lived a regimented life, which Claude attributed to Mortimer's days of service in the Navy.

"Maybe he stayed over at the Wamsutta Club after his evening meal. He may have made his way to the bank for his Monday morning meeting with the President, Mr. Willard," conjectured Claude. "I suggest you stay here, Mrs. Moriarity," continued Claude, "and I will make some inquiries at the bank, the club and even go to his office on the waterfront. You call any of those places and leave a message for me if he returns home and needs a ride. I will inform you in the event I learn of anything in my search."

Claude drove first to the side door of the bank. He noticed that the parking space for the president of the bank was empty. *That's strange,* thought Claude. *Maybe Mr. Willard was away and the morning meeting had been cancelled.* Claude approached the doorman of the bank and inquired after Mr. Weigand.

"The bank president arrived earlier and has proceeded to his office on the top floor of the bank. The chauffeur has taken the car on an errand. Lieutenant Weigand has not entered the bank," answered the doorman to Claude's inquiry. "I thought you were dropping him off," he continued.

"The lieutenant was not at home when I went to pick him up this morning. If Mr. Willard inquires about his absence, please let him know that I will be making inquiries at the Wamsutta Club and at his office," Claude informed the doorman.

When Claude arrived at the Wamsutta Club, he spoke to Mr. Oliver Green, the club manager.

"The lieutenant had his usual Sunday evening meal with us and punctually at eight o'clock left the club in one of the waiting taxis. His evening here was very predictable." Mr. Green told Claude.

Claude proceeded to the waterfront. The door to the building where his employer, Mr. Weigand, conducted his business was locked. Claude had been given a key and he unlocked the door and went up a narrow flight of stairs to the second floor. He unlocked the door into a large room that had once served as a storage area for raw materials that arrived by schooners prior to being delivered to mills and shops of nearby cities. A large door, from floor to ceiling, opened directly to the front of the building facing the waterfront and a block and tackle still hung from the stout beam protruding from the building. In a few hours from now, after the morning fish auctions, this room would become a beehive of activity. Three men, with their white shirt sleeves rolled up, would be tracking all the activities of the day. This information would then be analyzed by Mr. Weigand.

The room he had entered was dark as it had no exterior windows. A weak beam of light came into the room from the pane of glass on the door to Mr. Weigand's office. His employer's corner office had two large windows overlooking the waterfront and beams of sunlight flooded the room. As Claude opened the office door, he stopped in his tracks and a scream of fright escaped. He saw the lieutenant hanging from a beam. He observed the vacant eyes and a slightly blackened tongue protruding from his mouth. Claude put his hand over his own mouth trying to keep down what was coming up his throat. A breeze had entered the room as he opened the door and the body twisted a bit and Claude saw that Mr. Weigand had soiled himself.

In a sudden move he backed out of the office and ran down the stairs to the street below. He just made it to the corner at the front of the building when he retched and vomited the little that was in his stomach. He hadn't had time to have breakfast.

Bent over at the waist, Claude breathed in deeply, trying to compose himself. He crossed Center Street intending to go to the Cultivator Shoals Club nearby to seek some assistance. As he began climbing up the stairs of the small cast concrete building, Claude suddenly realized that the tavern would not be open that time of day. After a few moments, he decided to go to a ship chandler business a block away on the other side of Center Street. They were always busy this time of day getting ready to deliver supplies to fishing boats that were preparing to go out to get their catch. Seagulls were squawking above as two men were on the dock platform gathering supplies and placing them on an open truck.

"Is the boss around?" Claude tried to ask in as calm a tone as he could manage.

"He's in his office," answered one of the men. "Climb up this ladder to the platform and I'll show you the way."

Claude knocked on a door that displayed the name Kloger Bros. – Ship Chandlers.

"Come in." A deep voice called out.

The elderly man behind the desk was on the telephone and as he looked up to see Claude entering the office, he pointed to him that he would be with him shortly. After a few minutes of writing down a long list of whatever, the gentleman put the telephone back on its cradle.

"What can I do for you?" he asked.

"Do you know a Mr. Weigand who has an office just a block or so away from here?" Claude asked.

The gentleman nodded that he did.

"I'm his chauffeur," he continued.

Claude was struggling to get out the words. Noticing Claude's discomfort, the gentleman pointed to a chair.

"Have a seat. My name is Donald Kloger. My two brothers and I run this business. You look like you've seen a ghost."

At these words, Claude pressed his temples where he was experiencing a fierce throbbing. Slowly he started to speak.

"My name is Claude Lepage. I just found Mr. Weigand… hanging from a rafter in his office. Will you please call the police? There's a telephone in his office but I just can't get myself to go back in there. It's just gruesome. It made me sick to my stomach."

"Just sit there and I'll make a call to the police," stated Donald Kloger.

Claude was relieved when he heard Mr. Kloger telling the police that he and Mr. Weigand's chauffeur would be waiting for them on the sidewalk at the entrance of Mr. Weigand's office.

Two by Each
Chapter Three

Claude and Donald Kloger had just reached the side entrance of Lieutenant Weigand's office building when a New Bedford police vehicle drove down Center Street.

Two policemen exited the patrol car and approached Claude and Mr. Kloger.

"Were you the ones who called the station?" inquired the taller of the officers.

"I called," answered Mr. Kloger, "and we were instructed to meet you on the sidewalk."

Looking up and down the side of the building that faced Center Street, "Are there other entrances to this building?" inquired the officer.

Donald Kloger looked over to Claude Lepage who answered, "I presume there must be a back entrance. But this is the only entrance that I have ever used."

Upon receiving some brief instructions, the other officer, whose uniform fit snugly on his rather plump physique, proceeded down the street to the front of the building.

"My name is Sergeant Michael Griffith," stated the officer. "I've been given instructions that we should await here until our Chief Inspector arrives on the scene. He should be here shortly."

Just then an unmarked gray Chevrolet approached the group. A tall, lanky man with white side burns evident under his black fedora introduced himself, "I'm Inspector Daniel O'Malley."

He took out a note book from a pocket in his long trench coat. He began to take down information from Claude and Mr. Kloger.

The second policeman had evidently circled the building and informed the group, "There are two locked doors on the other side of the building and a loading dock at the rear."

Inspector O'Malley instructed, "Claude, please lead us into the building and to the discovery you made earlier."

In the meantime he had dismissed Mr. Kloger who had stated this was a very busy time of day for him and there was much to catch up with after this interruption.

Inspector O'Malley commented, "I notice that the door is not locked."

Claude answered, "When I ran out of the building in a fright, I never thought to lock the door behind me. It was locked when I arrived here earlier."

The stout policeman remained outside the entrance while the other three in the group climbed the narrow staircase to the second floor landing. The door into the larger room was ajar and after putting on a pair of gloves, Inspector O'Malley invited Claude into the room.

In a voice that was quite shaky, Claude pointed. "That is Mr. Weigand's office."

Inspector O'Malley slowly turned the knob and opened the door. As Claude sneaked a reluctant glance into the room, his eyes couldn't believe what he saw. The room was empty; nothing was hanging from the rafter in the center of the room.

"Mr. Weigand was hanging right there from that rafter," blurted out Claude and pointing to the beam in the center of the room. "What happened to him?" he continued.

Inspector O'Malley looked at Claude and said, "That is certainly a very good question. If what you related to me outdoors before we entered the building is true, this is quite an unexpected development. Your description of Mr. Weigand's body hanging in this room would necessitate that someone removed his body and all within a half hour since your report of his discovery."

Inspector O'Malley escorted Claude out of the office and into the adjacent large room. He instructed the officer, "Go call the Chief and ask him to send two more police officers to the scene. We need to secure the building and the neighborhood. Make sure no one enters or exits the building. When the coroner arrives, send him up immediately. We may not have a body but we need his forensic expertise to analyze this scene."

O'Malley escorted Claude to a chair and from the light coming from the opened office door, he found a pull string to a light on a side wall. The large room contained three small desks and files. Two large blackboards were attached to the inner front wall and wiped clean with lots of chalk dust on the floor below. O'Malley carefully moved about the room and found a staircase at the opposite end of the room.

A few minutes later David Rubin, the newly appointed coroner, made his appearance. The Inspector brought him up to date on the unusual circumstances of the case.

"I'm going to headquarters with Claude Lepage and I will send Detective Joe Barrett to assist you," instructed O'Malley.

Two by Each
Chapter Four

Inspector Daniel O'Malley gave a brief report to the recently appointed Chief of the New Bedford Police Department, Luke Guerney. Chief Guerney, who came from the city of Springfield, was still becoming acquainted with this larger and struggling mill city. He explained that Lieutenant Mortimer Weigand was the only son of an old whaling family – the Spooners. His mother had married a Mr. Weigand from New York. When they were divorced, Mortimer retained his father's name but his mother returned to her family name.

He frowned as O'Malley described the disappearance of Mr. Weigand's body.

"Are you sure that the observer of this incident is reliable?" he asked.

"Nothing so far indicates otherwise," answered O'Malley. "However, that's why I brought him down to the station for immediate questioning. We can't afford to have such a story circulating around the city if it turns out to be false. Will you send someone to Mr. Weigand's home on Mechanics Lane? Claude Lepage informed me that a Mrs. Moriarity was there awaiting some word about the whereabouts of her employer. After I finish questioning the witness, I will contact Mr. Anthony Willard, the President of the Whaling City National Bank. I know him from another homicide that we had here in New Bedford some years back. He's a crafty old man and also had some financial doings with the deceased mother of Mr. Weigand."

Claude Lepage stood up – almost at attention, when Inspector O'Malley entered the small interview room.

"Please be seated and be at ease," stated a smiling O'Malley. "I just want to get as much immediate recollection of the events that occurred this morning before they begin to blur. You have had quite a disturbing experience."

Claude related all that had happened earlier that morning prior to the discovery of Lieutenant Weigand. The Inspector took notes but did not interrupt Claude's statement, which was quite detailed. However, when he started to describe the opening of the office door and finding Mr. Weigand hanging in the center of the room, Claude was evidently shaking and his recollection was less precise.

Inspector O'Malley interrupted, "May I suggest something to you, Claude? It may help you to put some order and clarity to this horrible discovery you had earlier."

"Yes," answered Claude.

"Close your eyes and try to visualize the scene you came upon and try to bring back to your sensual memory what you observed," counseled O'Malley. "This may be very difficult for you. It's normal for us to want to forget or deny such a traumatic experience. But, it is important for us to have as much facts that are relevant to this case, if we are to solve this mystery. I'm right here with you."

Claude looked intensely at the inspector and being reassured he slowly closed his eyes.

"Try to breathe deeply and slowly," instructed the inspector. "What do you see as you open the first door on the second floor of the Mr. Weigand's office building?" continued O'Malley.

"The room is very dark except for the light coming from the hall window behind me and some light coming from the glass in Mr. Weigand's office door."

"Do you see or hear anything in that room?" continued O'Malley. "Take your time."

Claude answered, "The door hinges squealed as I opened the door. I think I heard a muffled sound and saw a brief shadow crossing the back of the room. But that may be only my imagination."

"That's fine," answered O'Malley. "What happened next?" asked the inspector.

Claude continued, "I entered the room and walked to the office door on the right. There was a dim light coming through the door window. When I opened the door, I blinked as the early morning sunshine from the two windows contrasted from the dark room in which I was standing. When I opened my eyes I saw Mr. Weigand hanging in the center of the room."

"Again this will be difficult but try your very best to visualize as many of the details you saw and heard as you opened the door," instructed O'Malley.

Claude continued in an unsteady voice, "After a few seconds I decided to enter the room. A dark rope was around his neck. It was strung across the beam in the center of the room and I could see that the other end of the rope was attached to something on a nearby wall."

That may be an important detail, thought O'Malley.

As Claude began to recall the sight he had of Mr. Weigand, he stated, "I don't know if I can continue. It's too gruesome."

"Take a deep breath," counseled O'Malley. Slowly Claude again described the face of Mr. Weigand and the fact that he had soiled himself. "When Mr. Weigand's body twisted a bit, I felt a breeze coming into the room."

Inspector O'Malley asked, "Did you hear anything at that time?"

"I don't think so," answered Claude.

"Could you see his hands?" asked O'Malley.

Slowly Claude recalled, "His hands were tied behind his back. I completely forgot that when I saw the conditions of his trousers."

"What about his clothing?" continued the inspector.

"He had his usual white shirt on. I can see his suit coat hanging over his desk chair on my left. He had light grey pants and his specially fitted shoes were on his feet just a few inches above the floor."

"Did you observe anything else in the room?" asked O'Malley, "anything odd or out of place."

"I don't think so. I just ran out of the room and building with my hand over my mouth."

"You may open your eyes, Claude. This recollection is very important," stated O'Malley. Relax and take deep breaths. I just have a few more questions. "How long have you been employed by Mr. Weigand?"

"A little over five years," answered Claude. "I had met him briefly at the time of his mother's funeral. My sister, Martha, who was the lieutenant's nurse in California was at home at the time of his mother's death and had introduced me to him. When he established his home here in New Bedford after completing medical rehabilitation in Salem, he contacted me and inquired as to whether I would be interested in being his chauffeur. He had learned from my sister, who continued to correspond with him from California, that I had just gotten married, still didn't have a full time job, and that I had been in the Navy Seabees serving in the Pacific during the war. I enjoyed working for him. He was very organized and reserved. Except for occasional conversations about our experiences in the Navy, he was quiet, hardworking and a fair employer. I knew very little of his work, except to get him to his appointments on time."

Inspector O'Malley reflected, *There are a lot of past connections in this case.* "You may go," stated O'Malley. "When I need to see you again, I will be in touch. You may want to go to see Mrs. Moriarity. Someone from the police department went to Mr. Weigand's home while I was interviewing you. I'm sure this will be very difficult for her."

Two by Each
Chapter Five

Inspector O'Malley dropped in on Police Chief Luke Guerney before leaving to meet with Mr. Anthony Willard at his office in the Whaling City National Bank. O'Malley brought the Chief up to date.

"With Claude Lepage recalling that Mr. Weigand's hands were tied behind his back, we have ruled out a suicide," commented the Chief. O'Malley agreed.

"What is strange in this case," stated O'Malley, "is that the body was removed after it had been observed by someone. I'm having a meeting with my detectives and investigators, including the coroner, later this afternoon. I'll give you a report of our findings."

The Police Chief told O'Malley that he had informed the Mayor of the situation. "I'll wait for your report before I give an official press conference."

Mr. Willard welcomed O'Malley as he entered his office and excused himself for not standing to greet him. "My hip is giving me a lot of pain this morning. My age and this damp weather are having its toll," commented the bank president.

Since the Inspector had already informed Mr. Willard in his telephone conversation about the nature of his visit, he quickly came to the issue at hand.

"I understand from Mr. Weigand's chauffeur that you had a meeting with him every Monday morning," started O'Malley.

"That's true," answered Mr. Willard. "We established that routine soon after he became one of my field agents."

"Can you explain to me the nature of his work?" inquired O'Malley.

"After the cotton mills moved south, our loan business supported some of the new seamstress type shops," explained the president. "Our bank has only slowly become invested in the fishing fleet and its support businesses. It always seemed a very risky business venture to me. Weather that is so unpredictable can have a devastating effect on our investment and not just the extreme calamity of a 1938 hurricane. Most of the fishermen have recently come from other countries like Nova Scotia and Norway with resources available to them from their native countries. We have had the unfortunate experience of having fishermen, who are indebted to the bank for a loan, suddenly leaving this port for a fishing expedition and never returning. As I said earlier it's a business with risk very different from an operation that is land based."

Mr. Willard continued, "That's why when Lieutenant Weigand approached me to assist him in finding a home in New Bedford, it occurred to me that he might serve me well by being in the field. He was an experienced seaman, a graduate of the Naval Academy. He also impressed me by how precise and deliberate he had become after his years in the service of his country. I sensed a certain affinity for him and, as my wife often mentioned, I treated him like the son I never had. It may be so but our relationship was always based on official business. From our previous contacts, I believe you appreciate that I do not leave such matters up to chance or emotions."

"What specifically did he do for you at the office near the waterfront?" asked O'Malley.

O'Malley sensed that Mr. Willard answered cautiously if not reluctantly. "For one thing the daily fish auction controls a lot of the finances of this business. There is a lot that transpires in those trades that is based on factors not easily comprehended by banking firms. The lieutenant spent close to six months studying that process and he became very keen to the intrigue that is part of that system. His reports were very helpful."

O'Malley finally reached the question that bothered him, "Do you have any suspicion as to why someone would want kill Mr. Weigand in his office and in such as violent manner? Had he uncovered some information that made him a target?"

O'Malley suddenly had a recollection of the initial experience he had had when he first interviewed Mr. Willard about the tailor, Mr. Beaumont.

The president's demeanor changed. He smiled but his answers were brief and somewhat caustic. "As you know well, I do not form opinions based on suspicions but on facts. There is nothing in our business dealings that I know of that would have put his life in danger."

O'Malley sensed that the interview was over. He did not want to further irritate the bank president. He was aware that his new police chief was not in a position to smooth over any missteps.

Two by Each
Chapter Six

Claude parked Mr. Weigand's Lincoln in a space about a block away from the former lieutenant's residence. Mechanic's Lane was one of the oldest very narrow roads, almost an alley, in this part of the city.

He entered the rear door to the kitchen where he found Mrs. Moriarity. She expressed relief at seeing him, "I'm so glad you are here. A man from the police department is still searching the house looking for clues as to Mr. Weigand's disappearance."

Claude suddenly realized that Mrs. Moriarity had not been informed of their employer's death and the circumstances surrounding it. Still shaken by his own experience, he wasn't sure how to relate the news of the lieutenant's death.

"Why don't you make us some tea?" asked Claude. "We'll sit around the kitchen table and I'll tell you what I have learned." While the tea kettle was heating up, Claude went to the front of the house and met Officer Robert Roderick.

"Mrs. Moriarity was kind enough to let me search the house before your arrival. I've made some observations but did not remove anything from the household." After giving Claude a few instructions, he left the premises.

Claude informed Mrs. Moriarity that Officer Roderick had completed his investigation and had left by the front door. "I locked the door behind him," said Claude, "and he made it a point to say that we keep the house locked and secure. Oh, he also asked me to tell you not to clean the house until the full investigation is over and to keep ourselves to the kitchen area when we are in the house."

Sitting across from each other at the kitchen table, Claude related that he had found Mr. Weigand's body in his office without going into any details.

"Poor Master Mortimer," exclaimed Mrs. Moriarity. "He had become such a fine gentleman. He is much too young. My daughter, Maureen, will be devastated. They were like brother and sister."

"What will happen to the house?" asked Mrs. Moriarity. And almost as an after- thought, "What will happen to our jobs?"

"The thought occurred to me," said Claude, "that I should call Mr. Willard at the bank and seek his opinion."

"That's a very good idea," ventured Mrs. Moriarity. "He's been involved with the financial affairs of the Spooner family for years."

Claude went into the front room and called Mr. Willard. Carol Walker, Mr. Willard's private secretary, indicated that he was busy in a meeting but under present circumstances, he had asked to be interrupted if anyone associated with Mr. Weigand called. "Mr. Lepage, I'm quite sure that he will take your call."

Mr. Willard came on the line within a few minutes. Claude told the president of the bank that the police had searched Mr. Weigand's home and had instructed him and Mrs. Moriarity not to disturb anything until the police department had made another inspection. "Mrs. Moriarity and I wonder as to what is our role in the household without Mr. Weigand?"

"That thought has also entered my mind," commented Mr. Willard. "As trustee of the estate, I would like both of you to continue in your employment. Set up a schedule between yourselves, so that someone is always at the house, including on Sunday. You may look after the exterior of the house and Mrs. Moriarity to the inside of the home. I will instruct my secretary, Carol, to have your wages ready for you to pick up every Friday morning until further notice. Cooperate with the police investigation and keep me informed."

Claude and Mrs. Moriarity quickly came to a decision that Claude would cover the house after he finished his work at the luncheonette at seven in the morning and Mrs. Moriarity would relieve him at seven in the evening. Claude expressed concern about Mrs. Moriarity being alone during the night hours. Mrs. Moriarity reassured him, "I've been up overnight for many years in the employ of Mrs. Spooner especially in the latter years of her life. I'll sleep during the day and a good book and cups of tea will make the evenings go by quickly."

While Mrs. Moriarity went to her apartment to fetch a few things for herself for her first evening shift, Claude inspected the house making sure all the windows were locked including the old wooden bulkhead that led to the cellar. He later called his wife Anne who would now be home from her day of teaching. He only informed her that due to special circumstances, he would be taking the seven o'clock bus home.

In the meantime, the group of investigators was gathering in the office of Inspector O'Malley. David Rubin, the coroner asked, "May I present my findings first? There are matters awaiting my attention back at the lab." The Inspector readily agreed. The coroner started listing his observations. "Without a body, I had to confine my forensic investigation to the premises. First, there was evidence of a rope on the top of the beam in the center of Mr. Weigand's office. The rope was oil stained, typical of those used around the docks. I have taken a sample of some of the fibers. I did not find any evidence of blood in either of the two rooms on the second floor. There was no other evidence in either room that would point to Mr. Weigand being present last evening, except for his coat hanging over the desk chair and a fancy black cane with a carved round handle made of ebony. I have taken those pieces of evidence and will check further for fingerprints. There were no signs in either stairway that someone was carried or dragged up or down the stairs. If what I have been informed is true, Mr. Weigand vanished in less than a half hour. That was quite a feat."

After the coroner excused himself, O'Malley asked for a report from Detective Joe Barrett. Joe started, "We conducted a search of the entire building, including the cellar and roof area, without finding a trace of the victim. We extended our search through the neighborhood and again found nothing. We quizzed some of the people who work in the area but no one saw anything suspicious. However, most people were just coming to the area after the incident occurred. We took the names and addresses of the three men who came around ten to work in Mr. Weigand's office. We informed them that the office would be closed today due to our investigation. Many inquired about the nature of our presence in the area but we avoided revealing anything until the Chief decides to make it public. The policemen in our group overheard many rumors but nothing close to what we are pursuing." Detective Barrett who was getting ready to retire commented, "I thought I had seen everything in my years on the police force. It's difficult for me to comprehend why a body, which had been seen by a third party, would be removed. This all seems rather strange."

Officer Roderick was asked to share his findings at the Weigand residence. The officer stated, "Mrs. Moriarity, the housekeeper and cook, was very cooperative. She knew and cared for Mr. Weigand in his early childhood into adulthood when she was in the employ of his mother, Mrs. Spooner. According to Mrs.

Moriarity, nothing was out of place. I looked through his briefcase and desk area and did not find a suicide note. I did observe two fancy canes in the closet of the front hall along with a walking stick normally used on hikes. Mrs. Moriarity informed me of Mortimer's injury during his time of service in the Pacific that affected his ability to walk. She mentioned that Mr. Weigand seemed to be experiencing more pain but never complained about it. She noticed it when he suddenly would close his eyes very tightly for a brief moment. She added that this was a habit that the young Mr. Weigand had formed when he experienced difficult situations as a young child."

Inspector O'Malley thanked his men for their reports and brought them up to date on his findings. When he described that Claude Lepage had remembered that Mr. Weigand's hands were tied behind his back, Officer Roderick interjected, "That's why I couldn't find a suicide note."

Detective Barrett added, "Initially, I thought that I might also find such a message. But the more I observed the scene there was little chance that he could have hung himself. There was no chair or stool upended nearby. A homicide fits the scene more accurately. However, the removal of the body approximately in a half hour mystifies me."

When O'Malley also related that Claude Lepage had seen that the rope was strung over the beam and tied to something on the wall, Detective Barrett jumped up from his chair. "That information is certainly helpful in producing a realistic timeline," added the detective. "Releasing the rope and lowering the body before removing it from the building would take much less time than untying the rope from the rafter above. To do so would have required a ladder or some such instrument. Again we found nothing of the sort on the second floor premises."

The Inspector informed his team, "I will ask the Chief to petition for a search warrant that would allow us to remove written materials from the files and desks in Mr. Weigand's office on the waterfront and at this home. One of the probable causes of Mr. Weigand's untimely death may be something he discovered in his studies of the fishing industry. Mr. Willard, the bank president who employed our victim, would not provide any theory or insight as to the reason for his death. Knowing the bank president as I do from a past case, he will use his own resources to uncover any trail that may explain this death. Along with being a trusted employee, Mr. Willard had personally become very fond of Mr. Weigand."

O'Malley added, "I will inform Mr. Anthony Willard that the operations at the office on the waterfront are to be suspended for the time being and to so inform the employees. He may resume operations but at a different locale. Both of you will continue your investigations - remembering that we are now not just looking for the body of Mr. Weigand but also a motive for his violent death."

Two by Each
Chapter Seven

The next day Inspector O'Malley visited the Wamsutta Club and spoke with Mr. Oliver Green, the manager. Mr. Green confirmed that Mr. Weigand had eaten his dinner at the Club with some of the members and, "He left us, as was his custom, at exactly eight o'clock. He took one of the cabs available at our front entrance waiting for a fare. Since he is so regimented there is always one waiting for him," said Mr. Green. "These days most members drive their own cars to the Club. Only a few retain a chauffeur."

O'Malley inquired, "Do you know what cab company might have picked up Mr. Weigand?"

Mr. Green answered, "We no longer provide a doorman to the Club. So I wouldn't know. When I do escort some of our guests to the service of a taxi, the cabs are usually blue in color. I believe the name of the company is Blue Bird."

O'Malley continued, "Would you be able to provide me the names of the members who dined with Mr. Weigand?"

"He dined with his usual Sunday evening companion, Mr. Anthony Willard from our local bank. And then they were joined by Mr. Charles Cosgrove, the owner of Cosgrove Marine. Mr. Cosgrove's company specializes in servicing the engines of the fishing boats and other machinery used in the fish processing plants."

"Would you know Mr. Weigand's normal routine after he left the Club on Sunday evenings?" asked the Inspector.

"All the conversations I have had with him indicated that he went directly to his home. If he varied from that routine on this past Sunday, I am not aware of it," answered Mr. Green.

O'Malley continued, "Did Mr. Weigand's dinner companions also leave at the same time?"

"No," answered the manager. "Mr. Willard stayed and played his usual evening of cards with other club members. I did see Mr. Cosgrove sitting at the dinner table with Mr. Willard having a glass of sherry after Mr. Weigand departed. I'm not sure when he left us. He doesn't enter the card room and normally leaves soon after dinner."

O'Malley went directly to the dispatch office of the Blue Bird Cab Company on Pleasant St. The dispatcher was familiar with the routine that had been established of sending at least two cabs to the Wamsutta Club on Sunday evenings between seven and nine o'clock. He looked at the records for Sunday and confirmed; "only one cab was at the front entrance of the Club at the start of the evening. Other cabs were dispatched later when they became available. There was an event at the Sharpshooters Club that night and our resources were stretched thin."

"It would be very helpful for me to know if any of the drivers of your cabs that night picked up Mr. Mortimer Weigand at the Club," stated O'Malley. "The sooner I have this information the better." He presented the dispatcher his card and instructed him to call his office and leave a message with his secretary.

The Inspector drove to the offices of Cosgrove Marine located south of the docks lined up with fishing vessels. O'Malley found that the small office at the front of the building was unoccupied, but a door to a noisy work area was opened. He saw three men busy at machinery and the pungent smell of oil filled his nostrils. One of the men pointed to Mr. Cosgrove who was inspecting some metal rods at the back of the building.

Mr. Cosgrove was able to confirm that he had dined at the Club on Sunday evening. "Mr. Weigand left some ten minutes before me," stated Mr. Cosgrove, "and that is all I know."

"Did you observe anything bothering him?" continued O'Malley.

"Why do you ask?"

"Mr. Weigand has gone missing," O'Malley stated truthfully. The morning paper had carried a brief story of a missing person near the waterfront but without providing a name or the circumstances surrounding the event.

"That is worrisome," answered Mr. Cosgrove. "I was a bit concerned when Mr. Weigand didn't make our meeting yesterday afternoon and without a word of explanation. He has always been extremely punctual and courteous."

"When I joined the two gentlemen for dinner there was a serious discussion going on between them," stated Mr. Cosgrove. "It ended abruptly as I took my seat at the table. We immediately began discussing the evening menu and all seemed quite normal except that I seemed to be the one keeping the conversation going between us. It wasn't exactly one of our typical light hearted evening soirees."

Since O'Malley was in the waterfront area of the city, he decided to go first to Mr. Weigand's office to see how matters were proceeding. He found Detective Joe Barrett placing the last of the contents from the office into a closed panel van. "We gathered all the material found in the two metal filing cabinets in the larger office space," stated the Detective. Pointing to the box that he had just placed in the van, Joe Barrett continued, "these are the papers and items found in Mr. Weigand's desk."

O'Malley informed the detective, "I'll recommend to the Chief that he conduct a press conference later today and identify that the former Lieutenant Weigand is the missing person described briefly in this morning's paper. We will encourage the readers to provide the police department with any helpful information. The fact of the hanging will not be made public. Except for Claude Lepage who discovered the body and the person or persons who committed this act and removed his body, only the police know of these details."

Detective Joe Barrett corrected the Inspector, "Mr. Kloger, the owner of the ship chandler business, was informed of this fact by Mr. Lepage and he has passed the word on to others. Some persons have approached our men seeking the gruesome details. The word is out and morbid curiosity is spreading as we speak."

"Thank you for that information," agreed O'Malley. "We'll have to provide the press a controlled version of the facts."

When O'Malley returned to his office in the police station on Union Street, his secretary informed him that the dispatcher from Blue Bird Cab had called and requested that he call him. He had some information for him that would be easier to explain personally rather than just leaving a message.

On the second ring O'Malley heard, "Blue Bird Cabs. How may I help you?"

When O'Malley identified himself, the dispatcher began to relate what he had learned. "Our drivers didn't provide transportation to Mr. Weigand this past Sunday evening. One of our cab drivers drove up to the Wamsutta about ten minutes after eight o'clock. Two men were standing near the entrance smoking cigarettes. When he asked them if Mr. Weigand was inside waiting for a cab, he was informed that Mr. Weigand had been waiting on the front porch of the club seemingly quite agitated and started to proceed to the sidewalk on County Street. A black vehicle approached him and the driver from the open window offered Mr. Weigand a ride which he accepted." O'Malley heard the sound of a telephone ringing and the dispatcher stated, "I have to break off now. Our other line is ringing."

O'Malley met briefly with Chief Guerney and they agreed to have a press conference at one-thirty in time to make the evening edition. "In the meantime I'll go to the home of Mr. Weigand and get a firsthand look at matters there."

"Let's meet in my office at one o'clock to discuss the latest report of your investigation," directed the Police Chief.

Two by Each

Book Two

Two by Each
Book Two
Chapter Eight

New Adventures

Chief Homicide Inspector, Daniel O'Malley, drove with his family to Dorchester. Every year they visited his elderly parents on a weekend prior to Christmas. Julia, the younger of his two daughters, was all excited. "We are sleeping over two whole nights," she exclaimed.

Her older sister, Margaret, asked, "Are we going to visit the Christmas window displays this year?"

Her mother, Maria, answered, "Your auntie Dee and I have plans for all of us girls to go shopping in downtown Boston on Saturday. We hope your Grannie will be able to join us. She's gotten much better ever since the doctors changed some of her medication. We'll leave the men at home."

A little after noontime on that Friday, the Daniel O'Malley family drove up Adams Street just north of Fields Corner. Julia shouted, "Look, there's Grandpa standing on the front porch waving at us." Daniel's father was a tall, lanky man. He had a dark overcoat on and a cap covered his balding head. The sky was overcast and the weathermen had predicted some snow showers later in the day. Michael O'Malley was all smiles as he welcomed them, grabbing both girls in warm embraces.

"Your mother has a small lunch ready for us," stated Michael, "we don't want to ruin our appetites for our dinner later."

Maureen, Daniel's mother, opened the front door inviting everyone in from the cold. "Your father has been out there on the porch for over an hour waiting for you to drive up to the house. He must be frozen," she stated. The visitors quickly settled into the two rooms prepared for them. Julia and Margaret always chose to stay in their father's room that he had used when living at home. Daniel and Maria used the guest room. The girls loved to look at all the photos and other items that their Grannie still kept in their daddy's room.

They gathered around the dining room table and quickly ate the sandwiches and salad that Grannie had prepared. The girls were especially excited to ride the Red Line train into Boston. This was an annual event. This year their Auntie Dee and Uncle Tony were joining them for a dinner downtown at the Union Oyster House. This was Grandpa's treat for Christmas.

Dressed warmly with scarfs and mittens, the O'Malley's walked to the Fields Corner station to take the T. Grandpa knew his way around and before long they were sitting in a warm coach clanking and screeching on the tracks leading to the downtown of Boston. Auntie Dee and Uncle Tony were waiting for them inside the front entrance next to the oyster bar made famous by Daniel Webster. Grandpa announced to the group, "Daniel Webster regularly ate at least six plates of oysters."

Margaret grimaced, "They look so awful."

Two by Each
Chapter Nine

Christmas at the Al and Janet Lepage household was a happy time for their three children. Only Charlotte, who was now in the sixth grade, sensed a certain stress among her parents. She had overheard some of the anxious conversations among them. It usually centered on money.

Janet had knit colorful woolen scarves for her two daughters, Charlotte and Louise, and mittens for all three. Al had been able to pick up a small used two-wheel bicycle and had given it a fresh coat of green paint. Their son Andrew, who had entered the first grade at St. Joseph's School, was ecstatic at receiving such a Christmas gift. The children's Christmas stockings had contained walnuts, oranges and the two girls received a new set of crayons. Al and Janet were happy to see the thrilled look in their girls' eyes as they inspected the colors of their crayons.

Most of the families that were on Al's bread route were also experiencing financially difficult times. The normal sale of ribbon candy and cookies that had augmented the Lepage income over the past holidays was down considerably.

Before returning to school in the New Year, Al and Janet had decided that Janet would return to work as a waitress at her brother's luncheonette. Al informed his children, "Now that you are all grown up and in school, Mommy will go back to work at your Uncle Raphael's restaurant. She will be leaving with me early in the morning before you get up for school."

Janet saw the confusion and fear in Charlotte's eyes. Janet tried to reassure her, "One of your aunts from downstairs will come to get you ready and off to school. I'll put together the clothes and other things you need for school the night before. I'll be home by the time school is over for the day. We'll have our supper together, do our homework and play some games as usual before going to bed and getting ready for another day."

"And on Saturdays," she continued, "we'll continue to go over to your Memere and Pepere and you can help feed the chickens and gather the eggs. And it looks like we'll be getting some snow, so you'll be able to slide down the hill on the side of Pepere's house."

"Oh, good!" said Andrew with excitement.

Janet's father had returned home from the hospital a few weeks after Thanksgiving. He had experienced a stroke, which left him partially paralyzed on his left side. He had learned to walk with a cane and for now, he was mainly confined to the first floor of the house. This was very difficult for him. He had worked long shifts in one of the clothing mills and most of his time off he spent outdoors in his garden and with his chickens. Janet's children running around the house on Saturdays had buoyed up his spirits. Plus Janet's mother appreciated the help around the house. They prepared some meals for the week, using the vegetables and tomato sauce that had been preserved in Mason jars in the fall.

Janet had also learned from her father how to kill and dress chickens. In the small room on the ground floor of the house that sloped down to Sassaquin pond, her father had taught her to place a chicken in a metal funnel with the head hanging out. The funnel kept the chicken and its wings secure while a sharp pointed knife inserted into the open beak started a flow of blood into a pail below. She would then place the chicken into boiling water for a few minutes, which helped loosen the feathers that she plucked clean and then singed the hair around the legs. She cut open the chicken and removed the innards, saving the heart, gizzard, and liver. This was not Janet's favorite task but one that needed to be done.

The new schedule at the Lepage household went fairly smoothly. The children got used to having their youngest aunt, Diane, who had graduated from high school the previous year get them ready for school. Charlotte was the only one, who feeling that she was old enough to take care of herself, expressed some resentment at being bossed around by someone not much older than she was. Janet tried to calm Charlotte, "You are a big girl. Try to help your aunt with your brother. Andrew can be a handful but you have a way with him."

Just before Christmas, Al had learned that Carl's fish and chips store only a few blocks away from the Paradise luncheonette was up for sale. His wheels started turning. His brother Claude had told him that his work at the home of former Lieutenant Mortimer Weigand was coming to an end. Mr. Anthony Willard had decided to rent out the house until there was some legal resolution to Mr. Weigand's death. Two months had already passed.

Al met with Claude after church the following Sunday. Quite excitedly, Al stated, "The business is only opened three days a week – Thursday, Friday, and Saturday. The owner, Carl Resendes, has gotten very sick and he can't do the work anymore. They serve an English batter, which is very popular. A woman from England who works with him brought the recipe from Liverpool and she is willing to stay on with a new owner. We could all help you get started."

"Wow!" exclaimed Claude. "I'm sure I could learn the technique of deep frying fish and chips rather quickly. Let me share this with Anne and her parents. This may be an answer to our prayers."

Two by Each
Chapter Ten

A few weeks into the New Year, Al asked Janet's parents if they could leave the children with them for a few hours. Al and Janet had planned a meeting with some of Al's family about a new business venture.

"We'll behave and help around the house just like you do, Mommy." Louise excitedly pointed out.

Andrew pointed out that he was big enough now to help bring the dishes into the kitchen from the dinner table.

"These children are a delight. Pepere can give directions from the back porch on how to clean the chicken coop. We'll get along just fine." Memere calmly reassured Janet,

Janet observed that Charlotte was quiet and hadn't joined in the enthusiastic display of her brother and sister. Charlotte was an intelligent and curious child. Janet reassured Charlotte, "Your father and I will share the outcome of our meeting with you when we return to bring you home."

Al picked up on Janet's statement, commenting, "Charlotte, from the little I've learned already about this fish and chip business, you and your brother and sister will also be able to help." This brought a smile to Charlotte's face along with a wrinkle on her forehead.

When Al and Janet drove up to the front of Carl's fish and chip store on the Avenue, they could see through the front windows that a few people were already in the store. Carl Resendes opened the door for them. A "closed" sign hanging in the windowpane of the door swung in the breeze. Claude and his wife Anne greeted them quite formally and with a sense of anxiety. Carl coughed slightly as he introduced a middle-aged rather plump woman, "This is Mrs. Mayfield. She has agreed to stay on and assist in the transition."

Mrs. Mayfield's bubbly personality immediately broke the tension in the room, "It's a pleasure meeting all you fine folks. You can call me Cora." A thick English accent, quite unfamiliar to these four French Canadians, greeted them. "I've loved working with Mr. Resendes. I'm hoping that he can slow down a bit and regain his strength."

Breathing in deeply and with some difficulty, Carl Resendes indicated, "I met Cora about ten years ago just after she moved from Liverpool in England. She was our new neighbor in the south end of the city. Whenever she cooked her fish and chips, the aroma would come wafting into our yard. When she invited my wife Maria and me to join her for dinner on a Friday evening, she served us her delicious fish and chip dinner. She explained that the batter was a long held family recipe."

Noticing that Mr. Resendes was struggling to catch his breath, Cora continued, "We started talking about opening a vacant restaurant on the Avenue. Mr. Resendes found and purchased two fryolators and a used potato peeler machine. I was put in charge of the kitchen and Maria took orders in the front room. I showed her how we wrapped up fish in newspapers back across the pond and placed the chips that most of you call French fries, into these short paper bags with the ends sticking out - ready for the eating. We clip off about an inch from these brown paper bags, open them and stack them into each other, ready to be filled with the chippies. The majority of the customers pick up these meals to be eaten with their families at home in the evening and others take them to their job for a quick hot lunch. Only a few folks eat their meals at the restaurant. As you can see we have only a few small tables."

"The New Bedford fishing boats bring in some of the best cod from the cold waters off the coast," Cora continued. "We coat a fillet of fresh cod by dipping it in the family recipe. The frying time and temperature of the oil need to be just right so that the fish is actually steamed under the protective layer of the batter. This results in flakes of pearly white cod glistening with moisture." Cora wiped her tongue over her smiling lips.

Having caught his breath Mr. Resendes added, "My brother, Miguel, owns a fishing boat. He provides some of the fresh cod but he also tells me what boat just arrived plus the price of the catch. He goes to the fish auction with me and helps in the selection. The size of the cod is very important so that the fillets are neither too thick nor too thin."

"We fillet our own fish," said Cora. "I personally supervise two women who used to work at a processing plant at the docks. We are only opened three days but we begin preparations on Wednesday and clean up thoroughly on Sunday. It requires a lot of work."

"Finding the right potatoes for the fried chippies is also extremely important," continued Cora. "I found that the local potatoes are not firm enough and too moist. A farm in Maine provides us our potatoes. Mr. Resendes drives up to the farm once a month and we store our supply in the cool cellar beneath us. During Lent, which is our busiest time, Mr. Resendes or one of his friends goes up every two weeks. We start peeling the potatoes on Wednesdays."

Mr. Resendes invited his guests into the kitchen area. He pointed to the fryolators, "These are drained out every week. Cora insists on this. Old grease can sometimes sour. One fryolator is used only for frying the fish. The other one we use for the chips. They moved into another back room, which was spotless. This is where most of the work is done. We have three areas for filleting the fish. We clean the fish only early in the morning and before eleven o'clock, Phillip Mello picks up the waste parts left over including the head, and skin. It's called gurry and some of it is used by lobsterman to bait their traps. I'm told that some is ground up and used for fertilizer. This area is always spotless before we start frying the fish and chips for the luncheon trade."

The four Lepages were all very attentive. Al could see himself driving up to Maine to get the potatoes. Claude felt confident that he could master the tricks of Cora's trade. Janet saw her role as an extension of her work at her brother's luncheonette. Only Anne was apprehensive. There was no way she could assist in the process of cleaning the fish. She could see her role taking orders at the front counter after school hours on Friday and all day Saturday. However, she was naturally shy.

Mr. Resendes moved to another back room. "This is the very important potato peeler machine." He pointed out the very rough interior of the large heavy metal bowl with a wide opening at the top. "The motor spins the potatoes around this tub with a constant flow of water. The rough inner side of the tub removes most of the peel from the potatoes. Each one is then inspected by hand, and any eyes or peels need to be removed. The peeled potatoes are then stored in these large barrels filled with water. We use these slicers to cut up the potatoes just before we need to fry them. As you can see everything has to be extremely fresh in order to have a successful fish and chip establishment."

Claude smiled and commented, "I wish we had had one of these when I worked in the kitchens while in the Navy. Most of my work was baking but everyone had to pitch in to peel potatoes."

Finally, Mr. Resendes pulled open a section of the floor near the potato peeler and latched it to the wall. He invited Claude and Al down the cellar stairs and showed them the many large bags of potatoes. "The cool cellar keeps the potatoes fresh but we have to check each one before we put them into the potato peeler. One rotten potato will destroy the whole batch. As you can see this business requires a lot of work but we have developed a steady trade, and with Mrs. Mayfield in the kitchen that should continue. If you are still interested, I can show you the books. We could meet with my accountant some afternoon. I understand both of you are busy in the mornings."

After a brief conversation with Anne and Janet, Al and Claude agreed to meet Mr. Resendes at the office of his accountant, Mr. Silber, at four o'clock on Monday.

Two by Each
Chapter Eleven

Al Lepage picked up his brother, Claude, and headed to the office of Mr. Silber on Central Avenue not far from where they lived in the north end of the city. Mr. Silber had converted the front parlor of his home into an office. The house was one of the few single family homes on the street. It was set back from the street with a front lawn and a cement walkway lead to the front door. A sign on the front lawn simply stated "Edward Silber - accountant." The house was in strict contrast with the three deckers whose front steps lined the sidewalk of the street.

A middle aged woman greeted them at the front entrance and led the Lepage brothers down a narrow hallway to Mr. Silber's office. Al was holding his cap in his hands, twisting it a bit. He was suddenly quite nervous and began to wonder whether he was getting his brother into something beyond their capabilities.

Mr. Silber was sitting in one of the chairs that had been circled together in one of the corners of the large room next to the bay window that looked out on the front lawn. He greeted the two young men warmly.

"Come join Mr. Resendes and me."

He rose and pointed to the two empty chairs. He pointed to the lady who had escorted them.

"This is my wife Gladys. She does most of the hard work in this office. She's the one that makes all the entries in our ledgers, calculates those long lines of numbers on our new adding machine and assures us that our double-entry accounting is accurate. She has the smaller desk loaded down with ledgers and pieces of paper of all sizes of which some are typed while others are written in ink or even in pencil. This is the material that our clients bring to us so that we can inform them as to the financial condition of their business enterprise. The majority of our clients are small family operations. My larger desk which at the moment only has a few reports on it is mine. It's a man's world."

Mr. Silber smiled as he looked at his wife who just waved it off with a quick shake of her head. She took a seat on the couch adjacent to the grouping of the men and opened a ruled note pad, ready to take notes of their meeting.

Al began to relax at this informality but he sensed that Mr. Resendes and his brother, Claude, were exhibiting signs of nervousness. His brother's right leg was jumping up and down. Claude hadn't experienced this nervous twitch in his brother in a long time – since they were kids. Mr. Resendes was coughing and trying to catch his breath. It was an important moment for both of them.

Mr. Silber started.

"Mr. Resendes has informed me of your interest in purchasing his restaurant on the Avenue. He tells me that one of you worked as a baker in the Navy during the war."

Claude acknowledged this fact by raising his hand.

He added, "I'm also presently baking for a luncheonette also located on the Avenue that is owned by Al's brother-in-law. Mrs. Mayfield has shown us the operation and with her guidance I feel quite confident that I'll be able to produce the same quality of fish and chips that has made Carl's restaurant one of the favorites."

Al continued the discussion.

"Mr. Resendes may have told you that I have my own home delivery bread route. Someone trusted me so that I could purchase this already established business. He knew that I was willing to work hard and he held the note that I was able to pay back in record time. My wife and family all pitched in, including my brother, Claude."

Mr. Resendes spoke up, "These young men need to know the financial status of my business so that they can be assured that their hard work will be successful. That's why we are here."

Mr. Silber went to his desk and returned with a long yellow note pad.

"I have put together a brief financial report of Carl's restaurant. He has run this operation for over seven years but I have limited my report to the last three years. The early years were the growing years but these last years have stabilized into a steady cash flow. There is an ebb and flow in this fish and chip business which requires some budgeting. The winter months are the busiest, especially during Lent. The summer months provide a smaller but steady income. However, when the mills and other related support services shut down for their annual vacation period, that's when following an annual budgeting strategy is critical."

He continued, "The food preparation industry is fraught with many uncertainties. The price of the major ingredients - fish and potatoes - can vary considerably even week to week. The price that Mr. Resendes charges for his meals can't fluctuate as much that frequently. The customers put aside a certain amount for these purchases and frequently don't have extra cash with them when they come to pick up their order. Even a few pennies increase in the price could be embarrassing and a steady customer could be lost. It is important to calculate a price that protects the owner and the customer."

Mr. Resendes nodded in agreement.

"It took us a while to figure out a price for our menu items that would allow us to make a steady profit. Normally, the prices of the products we use tend to go up. The weather will affect the price of our potatoes and during our busiest season winter storms can affect the landings of fresh cod. On a rare occasion prices have been known to actually go down. We reap that market only for a brief time for our customers quickly becomes aware of these changes. That's when we publicize a weekly special. We try to raise our prices only once a year."

Mr. Silber continued with his presentation.

"There are other major expenses in this as in any other business: vegetable oil, condiments such as ketchup, vinegar and salt, wages, taxes, fixed costs like rent and utilities and in your case, loan payments. Labor costs can be controlled by a heavy investment of time and effort by the owners. It requires a steady commitment."

Finally Mr. Silber reached the portion of his report that the Lepage brothers were waiting to hear. He stated, "Over a three year period Mr. Resendes has been able to realize an annual profit of eighteen percent after all his costs."

Al was impressed by these numbers; he knew that his margin of profit had decreased in the past two years to less than eleven percent.

Mr. Silber took two sheets of paper that were tucked into his yellow legal pad. He gave one to each of the brothers. He emphasized, "These numbers are for your eyes only. Each of the three columns represents the figures for the last three years. As I mentioned earlier, the gross sales vary slightly from one year to the other. The cost of items that I have highlighted in this brief report remain fairly constant except for the food products used in preparing the meals. Last year, as you can observe, the price of cod and the oil used in frying the fish and chips rose but the price of potatoes was lower. Maine experienced a bumper crop that year. Mr. Resendes lowered his labor costs by getting some additional help at the front counter on Saturdays from his two married daughters."

"At the bottom of the page in larger print," Mr. Silber pointed out, "is the sale price of Mr. Resendes business. It consists of the price of the equipment, such as the fryolators, tables and chairs and cash register. Another item is the present inventory, such as gallons of oil, potatoes stored in the cellar, paper bags etc. This inventory would be updated on the date of the sale. Finally, there is the price of what is called good will or the client base of this business. Establishing the value of this business is quite different than the home delivery business you own, Al. You provide a service to their homes and family. Here customers come literally off the streets to purchase a quality of product that they have come to like plus the friendly reception they receive from the owner and staff - good will. There is competition in every business and in your case, Al, one of your customers would have to personally discharge you from providing a service to them. In Mr. Resendes' restaurant business, a customer can just as easily go to a competitor down the street or change their eating habits without confronting him or changing their relationship with him personally. As you know well, Al, the core of a successful business is relationships."

Mr. Silber continued, "There is a new bank on Coffin Avenue that has expressed interest in providing the loan for a transfer of ownership. I have already approached them with these financial reports. What you need to do is put together your business plan and collateral for the loan. The bank will consider sweat equity but only to a point. Do you think you can provide this material for the bank's lending department?"

Claude looked to Al for assistance. This was new territory for him. Al suddenly remembered how dependent he had been on Skully for the purchase of his bread route. He quickly rejected the idea of seeking Skully's assistance. He had been fortunate in removing himself from the illegal numbers racket. He couldn't afford to bring his brother and the many other members of the family, who were ready to work and support this new business venture, into that kind of an arrangement.

"Would you be willing to help us put our piece of this transaction together?" Al inquired of Mr. Silber.

He answered, "It's unusual for me or anyone to represent two parties in such a case. There is always the danger of conflict of interest. Mr. Resendes is my client. He would need to be in agreement."

Answering the glance of Mr. Silber, Mr. Resendes answered, "I've only met Claude recently, but Al is well known to me and the local business community. He's a simple man, hardworking and true to his word. I would be willing to have you assist them and I trust that you will protect both of our interests."

Mr. Silber pondered these words for a while. He looked over to his wife Gladys. "Do you think you can free up some of your time to meet with these young men and assist them in putting together a business plan?"

Gladys walked to her desk and consulted her appointment book. They arranged a meeting for Wednesday afternoon.

Before leaving Mr. Silber's office, he asked the two young men, "Please give me the papers that I just handed to you. You should have memorized sufficient information so that you can have a meaningful discussion with your backers which seem to be other family members. Mr. Resendes has stated a very low price for good will which he is offering exclusively to you. He is proud of his accomplishments and feels assured that you will continue to manage a successful operation. He has three daughters, and as I mentioned two of them are married. None are interested, including his sons-in-law, in taking over the restaurant. They're all employed, except for the youngest daughter who lives at home. You might say that Mr. Resendes would be proud to have you continue his legacy."

Two by Each
Book Three

Chapter Twelve

Pursuing Leads

During the months that Mrs. Moriarity and Claude Lepage were caring for the home of the missing Lieutenant Mortimer Weigand, Chief Homicide Inspector Daniel O'Malley and his team of investigators had been exploring many potential clues to the lieutenant's mysterious disappearance but without success.

The inspector had quizzed the three men who worked for Mr. Weigand in the large room adjacent to his office. One had been assigned to track the daily fish auction, keeping records of each catch of the fishing boats that entered the New Bedford harbor. Before leaving on Friday he provided Mr. Weigand with a detailed account of the type of fish that had been landed, the price that each had commanded at the auction, which differed daily, and even per boat, and the number of pounds that were registered at the fish processing houses. Some of that information was provided at the public auction and others from the boat settlement firms that divided the proceeds to the owners of the boat, and then to the captain and crew. The division of these earnings, although fairly standard, could vary considerably with each vessel. The number of owners, the experience of the Captain or his relationship to the owner, were all factored in first before the remainder of the profits were distributed to the crew and even that could have a pecking order.

Another of Mr. Weigand's office members spent most of his time on the wharfs, observing and recording the daily arrival and departures of the fishing vessels. He also studied and examined the condition of each boat when they returned from a fishing trip, the work that was done on the vessel while it was in port and the condition it was in as it set out to sea. Some owners took great pride in their boats while other boats seemed to reflect the unkempt appearance and the wild and disorganized lives the captain and crew exhibited on shore.

The third member also spent the better part of his time on the docks, associating with people from the fish processing plants and other industries that serviced the fishing fleet. He had quickly learned to distinguish between the businesses that were run efficiently from those who were willing to cut corners and did a lot of backroom horse trading. The unloading and weighing in of the catch at a few of the processing plants was rampant with fraud. Some ship captains were known to accept a side arrangement that skimmed a few pounds off each basket weighed that affected the price of the load.

Detective Joe Barrett had studied the files that had been removed from the office and home of Mr. Weigand. He informed the inspector, "The files in the office on Center Street verify the account I received from the men who worked for Mr. Weigand. The reports were very detailed and often repetitive which made any change stand out clearly."

Joe Barrett continued, "Mr. Weigand evidently analyzed them on the weekend before meeting with the bank president, Mr. Anthony Willard, each Monday morning. The report that was found in his briefcase near the desk of his home was evidently prepared for that meeting. Together the two men would review the requests for new loans as well as those still outstanding. They had established a ranking system. The top ranking was easily approved for a loan. They ran a good business, paid their bills, kept their boats in shape. The owner was often the captain or the owner hired an experienced captain and disciplined crew. However, prior to awarding a new loan or extending a repayment plan, all the factors that were studied the prior week were reviewed. Had anything changed? Had the captain jumped ship to another boat? Did the vessel need extensive repairs after some mishap at sea? What was the size of the catch? The president of the Whaling City National Bank did not leave anything up to chance."

"That's in keeping with the bank president that I know," said O'Malley.

Joe continued, "The files in Mr. Weigand's desk drawer contained the reports that he had prepared for his prior Monday meetings. Everything was very orderly. In the report in his briefcase, as well as the two prior meetings, a few lines of the text were underlined and pointed to a concern that he had about the shortages in the catch of two boats. There is no further explanation. The rest of the reports are quite consistent and business like."

"I wonder whether Mr. Willard would provide some clarity to these concerns?" asked O'Malley. "He's not the most forthcoming person to question unless I can provide specific information. Have my secretary type out a copy of the last three reports with the areas underlined. Preserve the originals. Who knows? Someday they may be used as evidence."

Days and weeks were quickly passing with no break in the case. The hanging of a prominent person of the city on the waterfront had made for great press. Fortunately, a squabble between the Mayor and the City Council and other items of local interest were grabbing the headlines.

O'Malley directed, "Joe, set some time aside from the other cases you are working on and see if you can discover who picked up Mr. Weigand from the Wamsutta Club the Sunday night he went missing? Two men observed this incident when they were smoking on the front porch of the Club. Try to track them down, and I will set up an appointment with the bank president. I was told that he was returning from some brief time spent at his winter home in St. Petersburg, Florida."

Two by Each

Chapter Thirteen

Inspector O'Malley was able to schedule a meeting with Mr. Willard of the Whaling City National Bank on a Saturday morning at 9 a.m. sharp. Anthony Willard who had returned from Florida on Wednesday stated, "I will be extremely busy catching up on business matters after my absence from the bank. The best I can do for you, inspector, is to make myself available for an hour on Saturday morning."

O'Malley wasted no time presenting the three reports that the missing Mortimer Weigand had prepared for his Monday meetings with the bank president. O'Malley inquired, "A few lines in these reports are underlined. Can you explain to me the reason why Mr. Weigand would put special emphasis on these lines of his reports to you?"

Mr. Willard studied the reports carefully and pointed out, "I have not seen this latest report."

"The report was found in Mr. Weigand's briefcase at his home." O'Malley explained.

"All three reports refer to shortages in the catches of the Eagle and the Blue Spruce." Mr. Willard stated.

"Were these incidents particularly different from other parts of his reports?" O'Malley questioned.

"Shortages in the offloading of fish catches are fairly common. Mr. Weigand and I kept a close eye on them and we were always watching for trends. Mr. Weigand was alerting me to a possible trend. Both the Eagle and the Blue Spruce are owned by a group of investors whose personal identity is well hidden. Another matter, that is not too evident to the uneducated eye, is that the fish houses vary in each report. That is not typical. Certain fish houses are known in the industry for such transactions and only with specific captains or vessels. Mr. Weigand shared with me his suspicion that something was occurring between the time of the daily auction and the unloading of the catch at a fish house. His team in the field had spotted the inconsistencies but was still unaware of the manner in which it was being conducted." Mr. Willard answered.

Inspector O'Malley jumped to the question uppermost in his mind, "Would this discovery have been sufficient to bring harm to Mr. Weigand? Was he getting too close to discovering some sinister plan?"

Mr. Willard, who had been especially cooperative, expressed impatience, "Inspector, you know me well enough to realize that I do not speculate, and that I work only with facts. I know what Mr. Weigand was uncovering, what I would label a different business model. The best I can say from experience is that it normally presents a financial advantage to someone."

"Have you been able to discover the identity of this group of investors?" continued O'Malley.

"One of Mr. Weigand's team is assigned to this task," answered Mr. Willard. "So far we have some leads but little certainty. The investors are hidden within business structures or family trusts. If we discover anything, I will inform you."

O'Malley thanked the president of the bank for his time and returned to his office somewhat disappointed with the lack of progress in the case.

Detective Joe Barrett came into the office a little before noon with an equally flustered expression on his face. "I was successful in discovering the identity of the two men who saw Mr. Weigand enter a vehicle in front of the Wamsutta Club," he explained. "However, they were so taken up with Ted Williams being called back into active duty that the best both could remember was that Mr. Weigand accepted a ride in a dark vehicle!"

Two by Each
Chapter Fourteen

At nine o'clock sharp, Detective Joseph Barrett entered Chief Homicide Inspector Daniel O'Malley's office for their regularly scheduled Monday morning meeting. Joe Barrett reported on the various cases he had investigated over the past week. The last of the cases Joe reported on was that of Mortimer Weigand,

"I interviewed the three men who worked for Mr. Willard of the Whaling City National Bank under Mr. Weigand's supervision. I've personally reviewed and studied all the files taken from the office on the waterfront including those retrieved from his home. They shed very little light on the possible cause of their boss's brutal hanging. The collection of information at the docks was in keeping with their assignment of protecting the lending practices of the bank."

O'Malley asked, "Did you inquire about the areas of the reports that were underlined as part of Mr. Weigand's reports to Mr. Willard?"

"They confirmed that such discrepancies had been collected by them," Joe responded. "However, these deviations were part of a common practice that was prevalent in the fishing industry. They looked at it as creative bookkeeping."

O'Malley continued questioning his detective, "Were they aware of anything that may have led to Mr. Weigand's death?"

"Paul Santos, who was Mr. Weigand's eyes at the docks, did admit that he was often enough looked on with suspicion by some of the boat owners or fish house managers," answered Joe. "Some of these men were crude and slightly threatening but never put a hand on him. He did say that eventually the men who were unloading the boats and weighing the catch avoided answering his questions even at the bars after work. He had the impression that these men had been instructed to avoid him. He frequented many bars near the docks. He stated that the tavern called Cultivator Shoals Club just a block away from Mr. Weigand's office provided him the best information. Most of those who frequented that bar worked in the settlement offices nearby."

Joe concluded his report by saying, "All three of Mr. Weigand's men respected their boss and couldn't offer any reason as to why he was strung up in his office. They volunteered their belief that the work they did together was not the cause of his death and something quite unrelated to this work may have been the cause. They couldn't venture an opinion. Again they reiterated that Mr. Weigand was a gentleman, very disciplined, hardworking, and fair."

O'Malley thanked Joe and proposed a plan of action, "It has come to my attention that Mr. Willard who is in charge of the Spooner Family Trust has decided to rent Mortimer Weigand's home on Mechanic's Lane. Claude Lepage has been given notice that he is to be laid off and longtime employee, Mrs. Moriarity, has been offered a position in the Willard household. I would like to question both of them again and with you present. Let's interview Mr. Lepage here at the station but let's arrange to meet with Mrs. Moriarity at her home. Please arrange for these meetings sometime this week. This afternoon, I have another meeting with Mr. Willard at his office. I'm quite confident that he has his own people digging into the death of his employer. He wouldn't be taking this lightly nor is he limited in the tactics he may use to obtain information."

Two by Each
Chapter Fifteen

Carol Walker, the secretary of the bank president, greeted Inspector O'Malley warmly and escorted him to Mr. Willard's office. "He's expecting you and as usual you are punctual."

Mr. Willard rose from his large high back chair behind his desk with some difficulty. He took a folder from the corner of his desk and invited O'Malley to join him at a small conference table at one side of his office. O'Malley was pleasantly surprised by these actions. His past meetings had always been very formal and had consisted entirely of Mr. Willard answering O'Malley's questions. He never volunteered any unsought information.

Mr. Willard quickly took over the direction of the meeting. "Thank you for coming," he started. O'Malley reflected that he had been the one to request the meeting. *If I'm to get some helpful information, I'll follow his lead,* he decided.

"I have made my own inquiries into the disappearance of Mr. Weigand," began Mr. Willard. "His staff continues to gather information at the waterfront, but without Mortimer's analysis of the data it is not as helpful in making decisions about our lending. I didn't realize until he was gone that I had grown very fond of him. I could trust him not only to provide accurate information, but he would confront me if I suggested I'd use some of this material for my personal advantage. He was very different from my other employees or members of my board who discussed matters with me and gave me their opinions, but none ever dared to question my motives."

Mr. Willard continued, "Without acknowledging it directly to me, I suspect that Mortimer saw that I had grown cold and callous in my business dealings. My experiences with the cotton mills, where they would pick up stakes and move to southern states almost under the cover of darkness, had made me very suspicious. I suspect that he expected a better man in me. That last conversation we had together before dinner at the Wamsutta Club, that you previously brought to my attention and that had been observed by some as being contentious, was exactly of that nature."

Mr. Willard opened the folder that lay before him on the table. Inspector O'Malley recognized that he had never before seen this side of the bank president. He anxiously awaited the information that Mr. Willard seemed to be ready to share with him.

"We had both learned from different sources that a respected owner of one of the larger fish processing plants was having an affair and that the woman was pregnant," stated Mr. Willard. "My natural instinct was to find a way to use this information to a business advantage. Mortimer would not entertain such a thing and expressed disappointment in me and evidently I became visibly angry with him. Mortimer was reaching into a part of me that had become hardened over time. That was his final gift to me. And thus, it has become an obsession with me to uncover what happened to him. That's why I have decided to volunteer to share the results of my investigations with you and the New Bedford police department. And I hope you would keep me abreast of any developments that you may uncover."

Mr. Willard removed a typed sheet of paper from the folder and passed it to the inspector who sat to his right side at the table. O'Malley quickly scanned the two brief paragraphs and recognized a name that fit into what was previously referred to by Mr. Willard. "I need not emphasize that this information is highly confidential. I trust my secretary implicitly."

Mr. Willard continued, "My investigators, who do not seem to be aware if this liaison, have uncovered some other information that may be helpful in explaining why Mortimer is no longer with us."

Inspector O'Malley recognized that the bank president avoided the use of the words death or hanging in his descriptions of the situation. They were evidently too troublesome for him. O'Malley found it difficult to contain his curiosity and inquired, "What is the nature of their discoveries?"

"Be patient, inspector," answered Mr. Willard. Although emotionally involved in this matter, the bank president was still in charge. "This is difficult for me to tell to you, inspector, but Mortimer was experiencing renewed and terrible pain from the wounds he had received in the war. My investigators discovered that the physicians had ruled out any type of surgery fearful that Mortimer would become totally paralyzed from the waist down. They prescribed pain medication, which provided some relief. My investigators discovered that Mortimer supplemented this medication with drugs easily available to those who know the waterfront."

Mr. Willard removed another page from his folder and passed it to O'Malley. "This contains the names of Mortimer's contacts. The investigators have not found any reason or connection about these meetings and Mortimer's disappearance. However, we all know that violence is part of the trade. A deal gone bad, because of lack of payments, doesn't seem to me to be an issue since Mortimer had ample funds to support any additional need for pain relief. However, someone may have decided to get rich quickly. If they thought there were large funds available at the waterfront office, they were mistaken. That office only collected information. This is where I believe that you and your detectives, who are more familiar with the drug trade in this city, may be able to assist me in finding out what happened to Mortimer."

Inspector O'Malley was quite surprised with this new information. He reassured the bank president, "Mr. Willard, thank you for sharing this information with me. I'll admit to you that this is a completely new lead for us. We will be very circumspect in our investigations of this matter. I can see how important Mortimer is to you."

Two by Each
Chapter Sixteen

Claude Lepage was unaware that his right leg was jumping at a rapid rate as he sat in the bus that was taking him to the downtown police station for an interview with Chief Inspector O'Malley. He had spent hours the evening before discussing the new business venture before him. First, he joined Al and his parents in the front parlor of the first floor tenement, going over the pros and cons. All quickly agreed that the business venture was something that Claude could handle successfully. The overwhelming challenge was the financing.

Ever since the failure of his father's dairy in Acushnet during the years of the Depression, Mr. Lepage had been forced to mortgage the tenement house that he had inherited from his own father in order to pay off the creditors of his failed business. Only by the hard work of all the members of the family had they been able to be current on that loan. Collateral for the bank loan for the restaurant would not come from that source. It seemed quite evident to their uneducated financial minds that Al's business that was debt free would provide little or no assistance. Plus, Claude insisted that he did not want to threaten the security of his brother and his young family. Mrs. Lepage also agreed and quite emphatically. This was not her usual style but the tragic outcome of her husband's dairy and its effect on the family were still fresh.

Later he crossed the street to the home he shared with his wife Anne and her parents. Supper was waiting for him and as he ate, Mr. & Mrs. Saulnier and Anne sat around the table anxious to hear of the meetings he had had with the accountant as well as with his family. Anne questioned her husband, touching his elbow while he ate ravenously.

"What happened? Is it a possibility that you could own and run your own restaurant?" Anne was expressing the exciting dream that Claude had shared with her the night before.

Claude swallowed a mouthful of mashed potatoes and drank from the cold glass of milk. Sitting back in his chair, he started.

"Mr. Resendes has a very successful business and except for his present illness he would gladly continue running the restaurant. The numbers that the accountant shared were impressive. Al was able to confirm that from his own experience. Because of his admiration for Al, Mr. Resendes has offered a selling price much lower than what he would ask of another buyer. Our biggest challenge is that we need to get a bank loan and a down payment or at least collateral. That means we have to put something of value at risk with the bank, so that in the event the venture fails the bank can recoup their losses."

"Anne's mother and I have been talking and we have put some money aside in savings over the years. Anne is our only child and we are willing to provide most of those savings, small as they are, as some type of a down payment." Mr. Saulnier offered.

Anne's eyes filled as she reached across the table to touch her mother's hand.

"Are you sure?" she questioned. "You have done so much for us already. You have provided us a home. What if something happens to one of you?"

Anne's mother replied quickly, "We know that you and Claude will always be there for us. We feel secure."

After all these emotional discussions that lasted way beyond his usual bedtime, Claude hardly slept and had to rush out of the house to get to his baking job at the Paradis luncheonette on time. Suddenly his thoughts focused on the upcoming meeting at the police station. His last few days had been so preoccupied that the gruesome scene of Mr. Weigand hanging from the rafters of his office had faded into the background. The contrasting images flooding his mind were confusing and troublesome. He exited the bus a few blocks before Union Street so that he could compose himself while he walked the rest of the way. It was a cold, clear morning and he turned up the collar of his pea coat that he had brought home from his days in the Navy.

Detective Joe Barrett met Claude Lepage at the entrance of the police station. Claude had just finished smoking his Lucky Strike under one of the round police light fixtures that stood at each side of the doorway. He had been trying to cut down on his smoking but since the events of the weekend, he had found it increasingly difficult. So far, he had still been able to curtail smoking in the apartment he shared with his in-laws.

Inspector O'Malley greeted Claude warmly, "Thank you for agreeing to meet with us again. Detective Barrett and I have a few questions. As you know from articles in the press, we have not solved the homicide of your employer, Mr. Weigand. Have you any recollections or new information that may have come to mind that may be helpful in solving this case?"

Claude quickly explained that in recent days due to a new business opportunity, he had almost forgotten the incident. "I feel rather guilty that I have been so preoccupied with my own situation that I was no longer concerned about Mr. Weigand," he said.

Detective Barrett began and made a suggestion, "We know from your own statements that the morning you discovered Mr.

Weigand in his office that you were under considerable stress. You were concerned about your wife who had a recent miscarriage. Your dreams of starting a family together were suddenly dashed. Your wife's mental health was a concern to you. And then you discovered on that same morning that your employer who was so predictable was missing. You rushed off to locate him - going first to the bank, then to the Wamsutta Club and then finally to his office on the waterfront. Is there any chance that in this heightened sense of anxiety that you missed something quite obvious? And that it may have come back to you?"

Claude put his right hand to his mouth. Slowly he began to address the question put to him by the detective.

"Is it possible that I missed an evident clue that would explain his death? That is certainly possible."

Inspector O'Malley calmly joined the discussion, "You have gone over these details with me in the past. Let me try a different approach. Let me focus on the motive for the crime you found at the scene."

O'Malley was thinking of the information provided to him by the bank president about Mr. Weigand's addiction to drugs to help control his pain. The police department had still not investigated this new lead in the case. He wondered if Claude would provide any corroboration to this line of the investigation.

The inspector asked, "How long were you employed by Mr. Weigand?"

"Almost five years," answered Claude.

"What were your duties?" O'Malley continued.

"I drove him to his appointments, to his office, kept his fine auto in tip top shape. I also served as general handyman around his

70

home and assisted his housekeeper and cook, Mrs. Moriarity when my assistance was necessary."

"What was your schedule?" inquired O'Malley.

"I worked six days a week with Sundays off. Monday through Friday my hours were from seven in the morning to five in the evening. I picked up Mr. Weigand's Lincoln that was parked in a garage about a block away from his home, wiped it down of any dust or raindrops from the previous day and arrived at his front door at exactly seven-thirty. On weekdays, I would drive him home for his evening meal at five. All his meetings whether with Mr. Willard at the bank or any other business associates were planned within that schedule. There were no exceptions. On Saturdays, my schedule was more flexible. I was to make myself available from nine to five. That's when I assisted Mrs. Moriarity around the house, did any required shopping, had the car serviced but had to be always on the ready to drive Mr. Weigand to an appointment. On Saturday he regularly ate his lunch at the Wamsutta Club. From what I could gather, these were business luncheons. Upon our return from the club he would usually give me the rest of the day off. On Sunday, he would take a cab to the Club to meet with Mr. Willard for his dinner. That was Mrs. Moriarity's one evening off."

The detective asked the next question, "Can you provide us a list of the businesses and locations where he conducted his business meetings?"

"Yes, I'm sure," answered Claude. "There were at least a dozen. Some were weekly and others less frequently. Occasionally, there were new ones."

O'Malley continued, "Please provide this information to Detective Barrett after this meeting. Did Mr. Weigand ever speak with you about these meetings and the matter under discussions?"

"No," Claude answered without hesitation. "He was very professional in his dealings with others, he never gossiped and there was little small talk between us. It was mostly about the weather and matters dealing with the household. The fact that he always sat in the back seat of his beautiful Lincoln did not make conversations between us easy. And from my observation in the rear view mirror, he was always writing notes, reading his reports and the like."

O'Malley followed up, "What did you do while these meetings took place?"

Claude answered, "I mostly stayed outdoors and waited. I would wipe down the car. Talk with street vendors and the people of the neighborhoods. I never ventured far away from the Lincoln – always on the ready. During the cold weather I mostly waited in the lobby or front entrance of the building."

Detective Barrett inquired, "Would you say that over a three year period, you became quite familiar with some of the people associated with Mr. Weigand's business?"

"That is true," answered Claude. "I would say that I became acquainted with all of Mr. Weigand's business associates. Either when they greeted him at the entrance of a building, or more often when they would be leaving together after a meeting held in their business establishments or at the Wamsutta Club. Most were always very courteous to me and even more congenial than Mr. Weigand, inquiring about my family, commenting on the Red Sox, things like that."

Barrett continued his line of questioning, "As you waited for your employer, you must have become quite familiar with other employees, chauffeurs, secretaries, people like that."

"Not really," answered Claude. "First, Mr. Weigand was an exception. These businessmen drove their own vehicles. I would only meet some of the office personnel when they left or entered the building going on an errand. They all knew that I was Mr. Weigand's driver. My black outfit and his shiny Lincoln parked at the curb were a dead giveaway. From the grins on their faces, I often sensed that they considered me a holdover from ages past - an antique."

Inspector O'Malley asked the next question, "Did any of these meetings seem out of context with Mr. Weigand's ordinary line of business? Were you ever concerned about his safety? Did you ever feel uncomfortable?"

Claude thought for a while and rather reluctantly answered, "There was one place we went to occasionally that was away from the center of the city or the waterfront where all the other business meetings were held. It was south of the Berkshire Hathaway mills complex. It was a small brick building. There was noise of machinery, which I could hear from the outside of the building. There were no signs. And most strange for me was to see Mr. Weigand enter the establishment, in his fine attire, through a small door placed in one of the three large garage doors. These meetings were brief and over the years I only met one man who would exit the building for a smoke. He was covered with grease and wiped his hands always on a blue rag before lighting up. He didn't seem to speak much English. I believe is name is Paulo, maybe Pedro. He would go to the corner of the building, smoke his cigarette, and re-enter the building. Occasionally, he would nod to me."

Two by Each
Book Four

Two by Each
Book Four

Chapter Seventeen

The Bigger Picture

When the Japanese surrendered unconditionally to the United States on board the USS Missouri, a sense of euphoria had gripped the nation. The war that had been waged on both sides of the world was finally over. The entrance of US forces and the United States' ability to establish almost instantaneously a mighty military machine to support the Allies had been instrumental in liberating the European and African nations from the brutal expansionistic vision of Nazi Germany.

A proud nation had welcomed home the returning troops with gigantic parades of jubilation. Families were back together and the homeland was safe. The United States had gained a newly privileged status as a powerful nation that used its genius and its citizens in coming to the aid of others. There were some concerns, mostly among statesmen, that post-war negotiations in Europe were being threatened by a new menace - Communism. However, for the general public there was a sense of confidence that the might of words rather than the power of arms would be able to resolve such disputes. Nations had just learned a terrible lesson.

The war film *Stalag 17* was attracting large crowds to local theaters. When it opened at the Capitol Theater on the Avenue, Al's wife Janet and his mother were one of the first in line to get a ticket. Going to the movies on a Monday evening had become an almost sacred ritual for the two of them. Most frequently they would walk to the Baylies Square Theater just up the street from their home to view a latest movie and, of course, would purchase the latest individual piece of dishware to add to their collection.

Mrs. Lepage had readily agreed with Janet, "I can't wait for it to open at the Baylies. We'll leave a half hour earlier than usual and take the bus to the Capitol. One reviewer in the papers wrote that the film is even better than its original Broadway production."

Janet added, "And I just love that cynical smile of William Holden. Plus they write that Otto Preminger plays a contemptible camp commandant. I get scary goosebumps just imagining him in the role."

These few hours on a Monday evening were very special to these two women. The rest of their time and efforts were spent on the care of their large families. Now they were being entertained. Sitting in the theater, they relaxed and smiled to each other as they quietly slipped out of their shoes, hoping not to be observed. This had become a part of their ritual. They both breathed a sigh of relief.

The movie lived up to its reputation. There was intrigue as the American prisoners in the camp began to suspect that there was a spy among them. Sefton, played by William Holden, comes under suspicion. He is an enterprising and cynical prisoner who barters openly with the German guards for eggs, blankets and other luxuries. He organizes entertaining and profit making enterprises, including mouse races. He needs to discover the identity of the turncoat among them. He overhears a conversation in German between a guard and one of the prisoners, Price, played by Peter Graves.

In the barracks one night, Sefton accuses Price of being the spy and cunningly traps him in a major error. Price correctly answered the question, "When was Pearl Harbor?" but when Sefton quickly ask the time when he heard the news, without thinking Price answers six o'clock and that he was eating dinner. That was the time in Berlin, but not in Cleveland, Ohio, his declared hometown. The audience cheered when Price was thrown out into the yard with tin cans tied to his legs. Price was killed in a hail of bullets which created a diversion allowing Sefton to cut through barbed wire and escape. The movie ended with the whistling of "When Johnny Comes Marching Home." In the US this immensely popular song of the American Civil War had been revived by the Andrews Sisters to welcome the returning troops of World War II.

There was a steady whistling and humming of the song as the theatergoers left the Capitol. Mrs. Lepage could relate to this exuberance. Her Claude had come home safely from the Pacific and was soon to become the owner of his own restaurant. And her daughter Martha, who unfortunately was not close to home, was a happy nurse working at a Veterans Home on the West Coast. Almost weekly Martha wrote to her family long letters about her life away from home. And lately she was including photos she had taken with her new Kodak camera. Her friend Barbara was in almost all of the pictures. They had become friends way back during their nursing school days at St. Luke's Hospital.

While sitting in the bus on the way home, Mrs. Lepage sensed the sadness that was coming over Janet. She placed a gentle, calming hand on her knee. Janet's brother had not come marching home. Mrs. Lepage thought, "Maybe this wasn't the best selection of a movie after all."

Two by Each
Chapter Eighteen

After the movie, Janet and Mrs. Lepage walked silently down the street to where both lived. As the two Lepages turned into the small driveway between two triple deckers, one of Mrs. Lepage's younger sons, Jean Paul, was still outdoors wiping down the chrome on his shiny new automobile. He had been working steadily for the Domingos Medeiros Construction Company. He had learned the trade on the job. Starting as a laborer's assistant he had gradually become a carpenter. He could frame a new house, install windows, put on a roof and he was especially competent in doing interior finish work and installing cabinets. He took great pride in his work.

Over the last many years, he had saved his money and had finally had enough money to put a down payment on his new car that sported flashy tailfins.

"If you keep polishing that car, you're going to rub the paint right off." The car sparkled in the light from the back porch. Mrs. Lepage chided her son.

In the meantime Jean Paul's brother, Pierre, younger by less than a year was facing a very different reality in his life. He had enlisted in the army and was finishing his training at Fort Belvoir. Mrs. Lepage invited Janet into the first floor tenement for a cup of tea.

"We received a letter from Pierre today," she said. "Come in, we will read it together. I only briefly glanced at it. Pierre was never one with words and I'm not too sure what he is trying to tell us."

Over a steaming cup of tea, Janet read the one page letter to herself. Then looked at Mrs. Lepage.

"Let me read it out loud. Maybe, we can fill in the blanks together - focusing on the way Pierre spoke rather than his written words." She said.

Hi Pa & Ma and the rest of you guys.

We finished our training. It was rough. These Sergeants can really scream. I've put on eleven pounds and all muscle. I'll be the wrestling champ, when I get back home.

Some say we may be going overseas – probably a place called Korea.

Miss you, Peter. Pierre is too French around here.

The newsreel that played on the movie screen prior to the main feature had related that President Truman relieved General Douglas MacArthur of his command of US forces in Korea.

"MacArthur was such a hero when my Claude was in the Pacific. Why would the president treat him like that?" Mrs. Lepage reflected.

Janet shared her confusion, "It may have something to do with the fact that the Chinese are sending countless waves of troops into Korea. They are Communist and have joined the Soviet Union in supporting North Korea who doesn't seem to be content with the division of their country that was set up after the war. You would think everyone had had enough of this fighting."

Two by Each
Chapter Nineteen

A few blocks away from the Lepage home, William Normandin and his wife Meigan, were packing up their valise to return to their flat in South Boston. They had visited Bill's folks over the weekend and had stretched the visit to include Monday but now they had to rush back to Boston.

Some years earlier Bill had been sponsored by his then boss, Daniel O'Malley, to become a member of the Federal Bureau of Investigation. O'Malley was attending a graduation ceremony at his Alma Mater, Boston College, when he was approached by a recruiter for the FBI. A joint code-breaking effort between the US and the UK had confirmed the existence of Americans working in the United States for Soviet intelligence. Herbert Hoover, the FBI director, had received the go-ahead to expand the espionage division of the bureau.

John Byrnes, the recruiter, had been instructed to focus on Catholic colleges. The FBI director had become convinced that some of his best and most trustworthy agents came from this religious background, even though he himself was a Presbyterian and a devoted Freemason.

"May I have a word with you?" John asked O'Malley.

O'Malley excused himself as he drew away from the few friends who had been recalling their days at the college.

"My name is John Byrnes and I am with the FBI. My present assignment is to recruit new members for the Bureau. Inspector O'Malley, you come highly recommended to me. I've been advised that you would be able to advise and guide me in the selection of such a candidate."

O'Malley was taken totally by surprise with this request.

"I believe I am happy and proud to receive such a recommendation. However, I would need to know more about the assignment of this person, qualifications required for that position and so much more." He answered.

John Byrnes assured O'Malley that he would be able to satisfy all these questions.

"Would you be willing to explore this matter with me?"

The outcome of that brief conversation had completely changed William Normandin's life. He joined a group of thirty young men from around the country at a training academy in the DC area. It had entailed a twenty week course of intensive instruction focusing on academics, firearm training, operational skills and even case exercises. Fundamentals of law, ethics, investigative techniques and interrogation were part of a wide array of topics that needed to be mastered with a minimum requirement of 85%. Firearm training had included not only the use of a pistol but shotguns and submachine guns with a scoring of 80% or better on the qualification course. In addition to passing a series of physical fitness test, Bill had learned a variety of on-the-job skills, including disarming techniques, handcuffing, surveillance and intelligence gathering.

Upon the successful completion of his training, Bill Normandin had been assigned to the Boston Field Office. A few years later he was appointed as a Special Agent in the espionage division. While living in a flat that he shared with another agent in South Boston, Bill had first met Meigan Gillespie at a Friday night party. He had only spoken briefly with her but her smiling freckled face would flash into his memory at the strangest times. A few months later he took the initiative to track her down through one of his friends. She accepted an invitation to join him for dinner at an Italian restaurant in Boston's North End.

Less than six months later, the family members of Bill Normandin - small by traditional French-Canadian standards, attended the wedding of their son William and his bride Meigan. The congenial and approachable Father John Phelan, the recently appointed pastor of St. Ann's Parish in the Neponset neighborhood of Dorchester, presided over the ceremony. Bill had also invited his former boss and mentor, Daniel O'Malley and his wife Maria, to share this significant moment in his life.

At the reception, Daniel O'Malley quickly discovered that he was acquainted with some of the Gillespie family. One of Meigan's uncles had been a member of the same mounted police unit as his father. Standing tall with the help of his cane, Meigan's elderly relative, Patrick, smiled as he remembered.

"So you are little Danny, Michael's son. Your father and I had some great times together. How is he? I haven't been to any of our reunions lately." Pointing to his cane he continued, "I had a stroke a few years ago."

Daniel answered, "He manages well enough. My mother was quite ill some time ago. We thought we might lose her but my father took great care of her. They still live in their home on Adams Street."

"If I remember correctly, your mother was a nurse and a cute one. I had my eye on her but your father snatched her up before I could pop the question," stated Patrick. "I still remember our times together at Jacob Wirth's. After a day of riding our horses through the park and public garden, there was nothing better than sitting at their great mahogany bar and enjoying one of their gigantic Reuben sandwiches and an ice cold beer. I can still visualize the place with sawdust on the floor and Fritz in his white shirt, black bow tie and jacket with a white apron around his waist and a towel over his arm as he carried three or four mugs of beer in each of his large hands. I understand he's retired after spending close to sixty years on the job."

In one of their exchanges at the reception, Bill surprised O'Malley. Softly he posed a question.

"After my honeymoon, would you be willing to meet with me privately? I'm looking for some assistance in one of my assignments." A time and place was set. Daniel O'Malley drove home with Maria, his mind filled with curiosity.

Two by Each
Chapter Twenty

Special Agent William Normandin had taken the opportunity of another visit to his family to meet with Inspector O'Malley. Ever since their first meeting after his honeymoon, the two had met regularly over the past few years. Bill Normandin had given Daniel O'Malley a brief description of his special assignment.

"The military has provided enough intelligence to Congress to convince its members that Russia is developing a plan to invade and occupy the US territory of Alaska," stated Bill. "The military believes that it would be an airborne invasion involving bombing and the dropping of paratroopers. The most likely targets are thought to be Nome, Fairbanks, Anchorage and Seward. We are recruiting and training fishermen, bush pilots, even trappers across Alaska for a covert network to feed intelligence to our military. The plan is to have these citizen-agents ready to hide from the invaders and while in hiding transmit word of enemy movements. Established hiding places are being set up with survival caches of food, cold-weather gear, message-coding material and radios."

"This sounds to me similar to a plan used by the Japanese in their invasion of the islands of the South Pacific." O'Malley had reflected.

"That's true," answered Bill. "But there are two major differences. The Japanese planted their own military personnel as observers on the island they were occupying. In our case we are enlisting civilians as intelligence operatives on US soil."

Bill had clarified, "My special assignment is to draw up a similar plan to watch and protect a portion of our North Eastern seaboard. I have been recruiting fishermen, island dwellers off the coast and lighthouse keepers to serve in a similar capacity. The Canadian government is cooperating and supporting joint efforts on both sides of the continent. Together we will be covering the Bay of Fundy that lies between Maine and Nova Scotia. Our countries will be establishing a joint command post on the Grand Manan Island which is part of New Brunswick. Each country will cover their own shore but have agreed to share the gathered intelligence. On the East Coast the threat expected is not from the air but from the sea. The Russians are known to be increasing their submarine fleet. An invasion of our shores is not anticipated. However, there is danger of spies being dropped off our coasts and infiltrating onto the mainland."

At this present meeting held at Thad's Restaurant in the far north end of the city, Bill Normandin was particularly interested in getting the latest information on the mysterious disappearance of former Lieutenant Mortimer Spooner Weigand.

"For about a year now, Mortimer, who both of us knew quite well from another case, was assisting us in evaluating potential recruits for this clandestine mission. The knowledge he had accumulated about the New Bedford fishing fleet and the men who plied our rich coastal waters in search of ground fish and lobster was extensive and very reliable. Mortimer's strange death and disappearance is a great concern. We are concerned that our clandestine operation may have been infiltrated." Bill informed the inspector.

O'Malley was taken by surprise that Mortimer was part of Bill Normandin's special assignment. He briefly brought Bill up to speed as to the investigation.

"We continue to feel quite confident that the single viewing of Mr. Weigand's death by hanging in his dockside office is reliable.

We have made little progress in discovering his body. The latest lead that we are following is that Mortimer may have been involved in some illegal drug use. We are only beginning to explore that avenue of the investigation."

They had concluded their meeting over a piece of Thad's famous chocolate cake and coffee. They promised to share the names and location of the persons under their own separate investigation.

Two by Each
Book Five

Two by Each

Book Five

Chapter Twenty-one

New Revelations

On the way to the home of Mrs. Moriarity, Inspector O'Malley informed Detective Barrett of the information he had received from their former co-worker and now FBI agent, Bill Normandin.

"I don't have to emphasize to you that this clandestine operation is highly secretive. Other than you, Joe, the only other person I will share this with is Chief Luke Guerney. I have learned over the years never to leave my superior in the dark. One never knows when something unforeseen may occur. It's critical in our line of work that he have our backs"

"Matters are suddenly moving quickly in this case. Totally new and unexpected avenues of investigation have surfaced." Joe Barrett reflected.

O'Malley agreed, "That's why I want you to follow up on the information we received from Claude Lepage. Check out what seems to be a garage in the South End. When I meet with the Chief this afternoon, I hope to get a report on the names of drug traffickers provided to us by Mr. Willard at the bank."

Mrs. Moriarity greeted her visitors warmly but her usual composure was absent. She quickly informed them that she had declined the most gracious offer of Mr. Willard. Rather than accepting a position in his household in Dartmouth, she had decided to move in with her daughter, Maureen, in Maryland.

"As you can see, my home is in a bit of disarray," she stated. "I've done a lot of packing over the years especially for Mrs. Spooner. Every summer we trekked the family belongings for our time in Saratoga. And I helped her close up the house on County Street when she moved in to her new lodgings in Fairhaven. This putting together my own personal effects for a move to distant Maryland has me a bit shaken. It's the closing of a long chapter with so many memories."

"Thank you for agreeing to meet with us especially under these circumstances," started the inspector. "We will be brief. We are still investigating the mysterious disappearance of your most recent employer, Mr. Weigand. We wondered whether you could provide any additional and helpful clues. I'm sure that over the last few months that you have reviewed your long association with him. Has anything come to mind?"

Mrs. Moriarity moved a few wall hangings that had been placed on the couch and invited the two men to sit.

"I'm so sorry for being so inconsiderate. Please make yourselves comfortable while I go make us some tea. Where are my manners?"

She returned a few minutes later with a tray containing a pot of tea covered with an Irish linen tea pot cozy, three delicate tea cups and saucers and a plate of thin cookies. "I'm using my very best china that was stored on the top shelf. I was starting to pack them up for the move. They were rarely used. Isn't it something? We hardly ever find the occasion to use our best items."

Joe Barrett, who wasn't a tea drinker, graciously accepted her offering. He nervously held the cup and saucer knowing that these were precious items. He declined accepting one of the cookies presented to him - not sure that he could successfully balance another item in his hands.

Mrs. Moriarity sat back in the parlor chair near the couch.

"Now that's better," she said aloud to herself. "Yes, I have spent much time recalling my years with Mr. Weigand. Before my employment in his home on Mechanics Lane, he was always Mortimer to me. He had grown into quite the gentleman. His years in the Navy and, I believe, even his injuries and time of recovery had proven very beneficial. He continued to experience pain in his lower limbs and feet but he never complained. He was always kind and respectful. Always appreciative of what I did for him. He always complimented me on my cooking even though I knew that my simple meals hardly compared with the fancy fare of the Wamsutta Club."

Joe Barrett tried to direct the conversation to the reason for their visit. He was not as patient as O'Malley who usually allowed matters to develop.

"Have you any new ideas as to what happened to Mr. Weigand?"

"What keeps coming back to my mind," answered Mrs. Moriarity, "is that for the last few weeks before he went missing, Mr. Weigand was very quiet. He seemed very preoccupied. He seemed worried over something. He never spoke about this to me and of course it was not my place to inquire. On one occasion I thought that I saw evidence of the sullen Mortimer who had struggled so much in his youth. That was a bit frightening."

The conversation continued without any new revelations or recollections that seemed helpful to their investigation. When they took their leave, Inspector O'Malley offered to provide any assistance in the preparation of her move.

Mrs. Moriarity answered, "That is so kind of you, Inspector. However, I believe I have sufficient assistance. Both Claude and Mr. Bloom volunteered their services when they learned of my decision."

As they returned to the Police Station Joe Barrett commented, "We are getting more and more information from various sources that something out of the ordinary was happening in Mr. Weigand's life prior to this unexplained tragedy."

"Yes," agreed the inspector. "If we can piece some of these leads together, we may find the answer to this mystery. Let's keep digging."

Two by Each
Chapter Twenty-two

The next morning Detective Joe Barrett was surveying the exterior of the brick building that Claude Lepage had mentioned as the unusual place that his boss would occasionally visit. There were no signs on the building. It was about three garage doors wide. The center garage door had a smaller door within it for entry or exit. There were no windows on either side of the building whose length was about four times its width. The roof had slanted windows quite common in the local factory buildings that allowed natural light to enter the work areas. He couldn't explore the rear of the structure which was enclosed by a tall chained link type fence.

Joe Barrett approached the entry door and not finding any way to announce his presence knocked twice – the second time with more force. There was no response. He could hear some machinery type sounds within the building, so he tried the latch and somewhat to his surprise the door opened inward.

Upon entry, he announced his presence.

"Excuse me, I'm Detective Joseph Barrett."

A small group of men were busy at machinery equipped with a strong light above the work area. No one seemed to be able to hear him. He moved closer and tried to get the attention of one of the men. They all wore protective shields over their faces as shiny flashes of steel flew about the work area.

One man finally caught sight of him. He shut down his machine, lifted his mask to the top of his head and with a grunt of annoyance asked, "What you want?"

Over the noise, Joe Barrett again stated that he was a detective and that he had a few questions.

The man led the Detective back to the front exit. Once outside he took out and lit a cigarette. Barrett ventured a guess.

"Are you Pablo or maybe Pedro?"

This took the man by surprise.

"My name is Pablo. Why you ask?" He answered.

Barrett briefly explained that he was inquiring about a gentleman who had visited here recently and was now missing.

"I know nothing," Pablo answered. "I only work here. My boss is not here. He come every day about noon to check. Come back."

And just as quickly as his short statements, Pablo stamped out his cigarette and reentered the building.

Rather than returning to the station, Barrett decided to reconnoiter the area. He walked the shore front nearby. Except for a few other manufacturing type buildings, most of the area consisted of small family homes. Across the way looking over to Fairhaven, the Butler Flats lighthouse seemed strikingly close. Barrett remembered the stories his grandfather had told him about the light. The engineer-architect who built the lighthouse was also the one who had constructed the foundation of the Statue of Liberty. Its shiny white tower contrasted with the dark iron plates of the caisson which had been submerged another twelve feet at mean low water. The Baker family had been keepers of the light for over fifty years. Charles Baker, who had replaced his father as keeper, was alone at the lighthouse during the 1938 hurricane. Barrett remembered reading an account: *in the hurricane looking out… seeing it twist in the water.... The lighthouse never tipped. It must have a good anchor.*

Detective Barrett returned to his quest a few minutes after noon. He was encouraged to see that a newer vehicle was now parked directly in front of the building. Again no one answered his knock on the door, so he entered cautiously. A man with a black fedora was talking with Pablo.

They turned around to see him enter – the light from the open door had gotten their attention. The gentleman approached the detective.

"You have some questions," he stated. "Come to my office. It's too noisy in here."

The office was located at the rear of the building. It was small and dark with only one small window at shoulder height and strangely, to a detective, there was no other doorway than the one they had entered from the main work area. When the heavy door was closed behind them, it muffled the sound from that room. Once the man pulled on the light above them, he introduced himself.

"I'm Carlos Frias. And you are?"

Barrett took out his badge and stated, "I'm Detective Joseph Barrett from the downtown police station. I'm investigating the suspicious disappearance of Mr. Mortimer Weigand who we understand visited your premises on some occasions."

Mr. Frias commented, "I have read something about this in the papers. And, yes, we did have some business dealings together. Our main line of business is retrofitting fishing trawlers that had been commissioned during the last war by the Navy as minesweepers. Dragging for fish has grown increasingly more profitable. New Bedford has become an important port in this type of fishing because of our proximity to Georges Bank. The equipment is constantly being improved including the use of electronic aids. We specialize in the installation of radio navigation aids. These older vessels are unique and require the fabrication of special parts." Mr. Frias pointed to some metal pieces on a table that seemed to also serve as his desk.

"What was the nature of Mr. Weigand's business dealings with your company?" asked Barrett.

Mr. Frias answered, "He never purchased anything himself. He would keep abreast of the latest developments. Also he would direct some vessel owners to my shop. In some ways, he was an outside salesperson for me but without costing me a dime. It was a great arrangement."

Two by Each
Chapter Twenty-three

New Bedford Police Chief Luke Guerney welcomed Inspector O'Malley into his office. He was surprised that the inspector made the effort of removing an object that held the office door open and then had proceeded to close the door. The heat distribution in the old precinct building was quite uneven. The chief's corner office received the bulk of it. On this rather mild April morning the windows were cracked open and the open door helped to create some cross ventilation.

O'Malley explained the need for privacy.

"I've received some confidential information from the FBI."

He detailed his meeting with FBI Agent William Normandin. The Chief was aware that Bill Normandin had previously been a member of the inspector's team. The new Chief had taken over command after Bill's departure from the local police force.

Chief Guerney expressed irritation at not being previously informed of this clandestine operation.

"The FBI has been working in my jurisdiction and are only now bringing us up to speed. It's all too typical of how the Feds operate. Now that they need our assistance, they reveal their hand; and of course only as much as they want to tell us. Anyway let's cooperate in this investigation. On our part, let's be professional."

The Chief presented O'Malley with the report from the division that investigated the growing problem of illicit drugs coming into the city.

"Inspector Al Ramos has detailed the operations of the two men that the bank president gave you. They are well known on the waterfront. They are considered to be small time operators. The source of their contraband comes to the area by land and not by sea. There is evidence that a least one driver of the Hemingway Trucking Company moves the product up and down the coast. If you've been to New York City lately, you probably saw one of their large eighteen wheelers over one of the buildings. It's quite a creative way of advertising their trucking company. Our investigation does not reveal that the local owners of the trucking firm are complicit in this illegal trade. Our men knew that the Feds were keeping an eye on this operation since it has interstate implications. They didn't move in on it as they're always looking for the big fish."

After bringing the Chief up to date on the Mr. Weigand case and on two other homicides in the city, O'Malley went to his office to pick up his coat and hat. When Mrs. Moriarty mentioned that Claude and Mr. Bloom were helping in the packing of her belongings, it triggered a question in the inspector.

"Would Mr. Bloom be able to shed some light on this case?" He had set up an appointment to meet Mr. Bloom that afternoon.

Mr. Bloom was dressed in his chauffeur black uniform. This outfit was being phased out as chauffeurs were going the way of the trolleys. Most people were driving their own vehicles. The streets were crowded with new drivers and the police department had created a new traffic detail that was busy controlling the flow of traffic.

The inspector welcomed Mr. Bloom warmly. They hadn't met each other since the funeral of Mrs. Spooner, Mortimer Weigand's mother, many years earlier. Mr. Bloom was stooped over and no longer the straight arrow of his younger days when he had been part of the Spooner family staff.

O'Malley started, "I'm sure that you are aware that Mortimer Weigand is missing and seems to have met an untimely death. I was wondering if you might be able to shed some light on this matter."

Mr. Bloom answered, "I only saw Mr. Weigand on rare occasions. Occasionally, I would visit with Mrs. Moriarity on my day off. Usually, he was not at his home where she worked. I mostly met him when I drove Mr. and Mrs. Portnoy to an event at the Wamsutta Club. Mrs. Portnoy is quite sickly these days and they rarely make public appearances." He added smilingly, "We are all moving on."

O'Malley waited.

Mr. Bloom continued, "He would acknowledge my presence with a warm smile. We rarely spoke with each other. There was every indication that he was successful in his work. Mrs. Moriarity had confided in me that she was concerned about his mental health just a month or so before his disappearance."

O'Malley inquired, "Did you observe any of these signs, yourself? In his youth, you seemed to be the one that was most aware of these symptoms."

"No," answered Mr. Bloom. "As I mentioned, I had little contact with Mortimer and our infrequent conversations were very brief."

"Mr. Bloom, may I ask an unrelated question?" asked O'Malley.

Mr. Bloom looked surprised but nodded affirmatively.

"You had assisted Mrs. Spooner in the placing of Maureen's little daughter's remains behind the wall of the County Street residence," stated O'Malley. "It continues to confuse me as to why she never acknowledged its presence to me during my investigation nor move those remains when she moved away from the property. Can you enlighten me on this subject?"

Mr. Bloom hesitated but finally spoke, "I had been sworn to secrecy about this matter. That's a long time ago now. In the Spooner household, confidences were sacred. Without stating it explicitly, I believe Mrs. Spooner suspected that Maureen's daughter had been fathered by Mortimer. Just before Mortimer was leaving to go to the Naval Academy, I was driving Mrs. Spooner from one of her afternoon gatherings at the downtown park in Saratoga. We had arranged to pick up Mortimer and Maureen at the race track. When we approached the stable where they worked, we observed the two of them in a heated argument. This was totally out of the ordinary. They had become extremely close friends, more like brother and sister. When they observed us, they broke away from each other. Maureen accepted a ride home to the cottage. Mortimer walked away. When I approached him, he informed me that he would find his way home. Maureen who was normally happy and talkative didn't say a word the whole way back to the Spooner's summer cottage."

Mr. Bloom continued, "Mortimer left for the academy a few weeks later. His mood was dark. About a month later and just before leaving to return to New Bedford, Mrs. Moriarity revealed to Mrs. Spooner that her daughter Maureen was pregnant. I believe that is when Mrs. Spooner came to her conclusion."

"When we eventually closed up the house on County Street as part of her move to Fairhaven, I inquired about the precious remains. Similar to the young Mortimer she just avoided the question. Both had the ability of moving away from unpleasantries by sheer denial.

When we were driving out the driveway on the last day, Mrs. Spooner spoke aloud: "My little one has found a permanent home within the family."

Mr. Bloom added, "The will of the sea captain Anthony Spooner who had built the house on County Street specified that it was to remain in the Spooner family in perpetuity."

Two by Each
Chapter Twenty-four

Detective Joe Barrett reported his findings to O'Malley the following morning. He offered his conclusion.

"The operations within the building in the South End of the city seem to exclude any connection with it being a source of drugs as we first suspected. However, it may point to the clandestine operation of the FBI. Fitting fishing trawlers with the new electronic aids would be essential to the project of surveillance that is part of that operation."

Inspector O'Malley shared the report on drug activities on the waterfront with Barrett, "Check out the two small time operators identified in the report. See if you can pick any clues that would have precipitated the untimely death of Mr. Weigand. In the meantime, I will make another effort into identifying the vehicle that picked him up at the Wamsutta. Quite surely, there is some connection with this very unusual event and the disappearance of our victim. I'm quite confident that Mr. Weigand, even in a state of frustration and impatience, would not take a ride from a total stranger."

In the quiet of his office, O'Malley reviewed his notes from prior inquiries at the Wamsutta Club. He noted that the two men who had been present at the front entrance stated that there were no cabs waiting at the entrance. Mr. Weigand had expressed his irritation in a manner quite out of character with his usual refined presence. He had stomped down to one of the main gates on County Street. It was there that he had been seen entering a dark vehicle. It was heading south.

O'Malley thought to himself, There are three possible scenarios to this dilemma. First, someone from the Wamsutta could have exited from the parking lot behind the building, taken a right onto Union Street and an immediate right onto County heading south. Such a person would be known to Mr. Weigand. Second, another cab company with black vehicles had driven by and picked up a fare on the side of the road. Third, one of Mr. Weigand's associates was driving by at the moment and offered him a ride.

It seemed to O'Malley that the key to a possible identifying of the vehicle was that it was travelling south.

His investigation at the Wamsutta Club later that day was not helpful. Mr. Green, the manager, had indicated that only a few guests had been present that evening. There were many other activities and events going on in the city. Those who had parked behind the Club owned the more modern looking vehicles that sported fashionable bright colors.

One cab company owned black vehicles. There were no records that a fare had been picked up in front of the Wamsutta Club. O'Malley discovered that one of Mr. Weigand's business associates lived in the South End of the city and owned a black vehicle. O'Malley hoped that he had finally made a slight breakthrough. Mr. Arthur Lerner owned two fishing boats and was also the skipper. He was a regular member of the fish auction. He was well known for being a crafty negotiator. He learned that Mr. Lerner's boats were both in port. He arranged to meet Mr. Lerner at his home that evening. O'Malley was on a quest. Plus, he had learned that one of Mr. Lerner's boats, the Puffin, was being made ready for sailing out of port in the next few days.

Inspector O'Malley had made it a practice to be home for the evening meal with his family. His wife Maria would have everything ready for six o'clock. Both daughters, Julia and

Margaret, would join them. As usual O'Malley was very punctual. He kissed Maria as he entered the dining room. He then removed his suit coat, laid it on the back of a chair, and went upstairs to wash his hands. Margaret who was now in her final year of college was studying in her room and Julia with her red hair in rollers came rushing out of her room and squeezed her father saying, "I have a date tonight."

Maria called from below, "Come on down. Supper is ready."

As Margaret joined them in the hallway she presented her father with the side of her cheek seeking a kiss. All three went down the stairs together and O'Malley was happy. He also reflected on how different his girls were from each other.

Julia as usual was all excited, talking non-stop. When O'Malley bent his head for prayer, Julia could hardly contain herself for those brief moments. Once O'Malley signed himself with the cross, she just about exploded in relief.

Two by Each
Chapter Twenty-five

Arthur Lerner lived in one of the seven-room cottages that remained of the Howland Mill Village. The village had been a creation of William Howland who believed he could provide a pleasant living environment for his mill workers. He had especially wanted to buck the trend of other factory-owned worker housing that was commonplace in New Bedford. Where other developments were mainly a series of tenements constructed in a monotonous repetition, this village consisted of single family homes that allowed for small gardens and some privacy. These cottages had been placed on winding roads. Some of the original paths that had wound through the village were still in evidence.

Inspector O'Malley drove by Hazelwood Park that bordered this housing complex. The view of Clarks Cove that was covered by a variegated red sky from the setting sun caught his attention. Since he was a few minutes early, he slowed down and took time to appreciate this awe inspiring scene.

Mrs. Lerner greeted O'Malley at the front door welcoming him to join her and her husband in a small enclosed porch at the side of the house. The Lerners had also been viewing the setting sun. The red coloring was disappearing as dusk was now advancing quickly. O'Malley observed that Mrs. Lerner appeared much younger than her husband. After a brief greeting, Mrs. Lerner joined her husband on a wicker couch covered with bright flowery cushions. She affectionately touched her husband's shoulder and looked smilingly at him.

Arthur Lerner made it quickly obvious that this meeting with the inspector would be informal and casual.

"Inspector, you can call me, Arthur. This is Jeannine. We have been married just over a year. My first wife died in childbirth some years ago. How may I address you?"

O'Malley answered, "You may call me, Danny."

This was quite a departure from the norm. Only family members addressed him as Danny. In most of his dealings with the public, he was referred to as Inspector or O'Malley.

"Now, how may I help you?" asked Arthur.

"I believe you are an acquaintance of Mr. Weigand," stated O'Malley.

Arthur acknowledged the comment with a nod.

O'Malley continued, "Do you have any recollection of picking up Mr. Weigand on County Street in front of the Wamsutta Club a few Sundays ago?"

"Yes, I do," answered Arthur. "He's a bit of a strange guy. He is quite formal. I had to insist that he sit in the front seat with me. He was preparing to sit in the rear of my vehicle just as he would do with his chauffeur. But I like the guy. He keeps his word."

O'Malley queried, "You do know that he has gone missing?"

Arthur replied, "I was away on a fishing trip when this news made the papers. It was still a piece of conversation around the waterfront when I returned. My dealings with Mort were minimal. I haven't given it much thought."

"Are you willing to tell me where you brought Mortimer Weigand that evening?" asked O'Malley.

"No trouble at all," responded Arthur who seemed aggravated by this dragged out type of questioning. "I turned down

Spring Street and brought him to his office. He said little along the way and assured me that he would find his way home after attending to some business matters. He was perturbed to see some light coming from his corner office on the second floor, saying: 'They forgot to put out the lights again." I waited until he unlocked the side door and closed it behind him before continuing my original trip home. That was the last time I saw him."

During this conversation Mrs. Lerner had continued to brush up against her husband even placing a hand on his knee. O'Malley and his Irish heritage found these open signs of affection a bit distracting.

Arthur brought the interview to a quick end. "If you have no further questions, Danny, I need to get my rest. The Puffin is ready and we are scheduled to leave tomorrow morning. As the sunset indicates, we have some fine weather before us."

Two by Each
Book Six

Two by Each
Book Six

Chapter Twenty-six

In the background

Claude and Anne were sitting at the dining room table. Earlier that Sunday morning they had attended the eight o'clock Mass at St. Joseph's Church. Afterwards, they had spent the better part of the day at the restaurant. Two of Claude's sisters had helped them give the place a thorough cleaning. They had just completed another week as proud owners of Claude and Anne's Fish & Chips.

"Another week under our belt," said Claude with a broad smile on his face. "We all continue to learn a lot. How do you feel about your work at the front counter?"

Anne answered, "Fridays are a disaster. As you know, I come home those nights a wreck. As much as Janet instructs me and encourages me, I don't transition smoothly from my day in the classroom. And the pace on Friday evenings is always so hectic. On Saturdays, I seem to fall into a routine. I actually find myself smiling at our patrons as I take their orders."

Claude added, "Cora Mayfield is a dynamo. After filleting all that cod every morning, she is at my side at the two fry-o-lators keeping a close eye on me as I cook the fries and occasionally she allows me to fry the fish. I thought sure that the two barrels of peeled potatoes would be more than enough this past week but by Saturday morning we had to prepare another barrel. Cora alerted me that with Ash Wednesday coming in a few weeks, we'll have to almost double the preparations."

Anne's parents had gone out to a local restaurant for their Sunday evening dinner. So many people continued to play a part in making their business a success. Each evening Anne's mother had counted the receipts, making bundles of the bills, mostly ones and fives, and rolling up the coins. She then prepared a drawer of change for the following day. Janet had come over from across the street and instructed Mrs. Saulnier in these critical elements of managing a successful business. Janet had shown her how to prepare a deposit that would be brought to the bank on Monday morning. Individual envelopes were prepared to pay the employees. And other funds were set aside to pay the bills. With a lot of free help from family members, the business was making a small profit.

Looking at these numbers, Claude smiled at Anne, "We can't give up our day jobs yet. It's a good thing you have your teaching job and I can still work the early morning baking shift four days a week."

Across the street Charlotte, the eldest of Al and Janet's children, was reviewing the work that she and her sister Louise had done to help her Uncle Claude's new restaurant.

"I think we have to start doing our work of preparing the bags for chips and the newspapers for the fish as early as Monday. We'll do our homework right after we get home from school and then after supper we'll start these projects." She quite seriously told Louise.

Andrew who was almost eight was listening nearby. "I want to help, too," he stated.

"Well, you certainly can't help in cutting off the top of the paper bags with scissors or slicing the pages of the newspaper with a knife," observed Charlotte. "You're much too clumsy for those jobs. You can try opening the bags and stacking them into each other. You have to keep your hands clean and out of your mouth."

As she thought again, Charlotte added, "Since we ran out of newspapers, I think we'll ask mom and dad if we can get newspapers from the neighbors."

Andrew liked that idea.

"We can use my red wagon and we can go up and down the street to pick them up," he said proudly.

Charlotte looked up at him with a surprised look on her face.

"That's a great idea, Andrew."

Louise got into the mood of this part of the planning.

"I can go along and help Andrew. You can help Ma with the dishes and cleaning the house," she added. She hated those jobs.

While the children were seriously discussing their plans, they heard the familiar quick steps of their father coming up the stairs. They broke away and came rushing to greet him at the door. They had missed him. On Sundays he was always a part of their day. This day he had made a drive to Maine to pick up an order of potatoes. Mr. Resendes had left with their father right after the eight o'clock Mass.

Together the children started asking many questions. Janet interrupted them.

"Give your father a chance to catch his breath and clean up a bit. We'll sit around the table with him as he eats his supper."

A few minutes later Al was telling Janet and his children about his trip.

"It's a long ride and I paid close attention so that I can find my way there again. I don't think Mr. Resendes will go with me but one more time. He introduced me to two farmers from whom he gets the potatoes. They reminded me of your Uncle Robert's friend, Larry, who served with him in the army. They have the same strange accent and are very nice." Looking at Janet, "I was a bit concerned about the truck. It ran well but the weight of ten one hundred pound bags of potatoes is much heavier than the bread I carry each day. I could see the truck sagging lower as I placed another bag into it. I tried to spread them out so as to balance off the load. I'm going to have the springs on the truck checked and also the rear tires."

Andrew popped an interesting question.

"Can we go with you on the next trip to get the potatoes? We are off from school on Sundays."

Al answered, "I was thinking exactly about that as I was driving home. You would have to sit on the sacks of potatoes on the way home."

Janet chimed in, "They'll be no Sunday clothes worn for that trip and I can prepare a picnic basket."

Everyone was thrilled.

Downstairs, the younger Lepage girls were watching the *Ed Sullivan Show* on the family's new television. After the program they went to their bedroom and they excitingly continued to talk about the latest news that their sister, Martha, would be travelling home from San Francisco. They hadn't seen her in over two years. Mrs. Lepage had told them that Martha and her best friend, Barbara, would be travelling home by train. Martha and Barbara had completed their commitment to work at the Veterans Home. Both had decided to return home and find employment closer to their families. There was a lot of excitement in the Lepage households that night.

Two by Each
Chapter Twenty-seven

Paul LaMontagne was tending bar at his father's bar and grill, The Barn. It was early in the evening, still a few hours before the show would appear behind him on the stage. He was discussing intently the progress of the Stanley Cup finals with two workmen sitting at the bar. Gary and Alden were regulars who stopped in for a cold draft of Rupert's Knickerbocker after a day's work at the Blue Stone Quarry.

The Bruins, who had defeated the defending champs the Detroit Red Wings to reach the finals, had beaten the Montreal Canadiens at the Forum in Montreal to even off the series, 1 to 1. They were returning to the Boston Garden for the next two games.

Alden was saying, "We've found an answer to Montreal's scoring machine. Our goalies were able to stop Maurice the 'Rocket' Richard and what is left of their famous 'Punch Line.'"

Gary added, "Milt Schmidt's goal in the final minutes of the game shows that he isn't ready for the retirement farm. The Bruins have their own 'Kraut Line' with him at the center. He's a superb stickhandler and a smooth playmaker that was able to penetrate Montreal's defense. Now that we are on our home ice, we should be able to take revenge for our lost to them last year in the semi-finals."

As he was wiping down the bar, Paul stated, "I would just about give my shirt to get tickets for one of those games at the Garden."

Gary said, "Our foreman was saying that he knew that one of the bosses in the office was trying to sell two tickets for the fourth game. They'll cost a pretty penny. Do you want me to check it out?"

Paul nodded, "Sure. No harm in asking."

Gary looked at the clock at the side of the raised stage behind the bar and said, "Give me the phone. I'll call the office at the Quarry. Joe's usually there after our day's work planning the schedule for tomorrow."

Paul pulled the phone from under the bar and placed it before Gary and then went to the right end of the bar to serve other regulars who had just entered the building. The sunlight had broken into the darkened room as the door opened and closed.

Gary called out, "Paul, you can have them at $45.00 a ticket and you have to take both."

Without flinching at the steep price, Paul replied back. "It's a go."

As Paul returned to place the phone back under the bar, he began to have second thoughts. His wife Claudia would be upset. Ever since the contracting work at Fort Rodman had come to an end, the family budget had been tight. He was doing some carpentry work on his own during the day and tending his father's bar at night. The carpentry work was good money but spotty. It was no longer that former steady paycheck that had allowed him to have his play money.

Also he needed to find someone to join him. He quickly thought of his brothers-in-law, one of the Lepages. That would also help with convincing Claudia that this was a good idea, a once in a million. He didn't think he could persuade the older brothers - Al and Claude. They were too busily invested in the new fish and chip restaurant. Then it struck him. The younger Pierre was home on leave and he was a rabid sports fan. Now all he needed was the money.

And so a few nights later Pierre was sitting in the front seat of Paul's shiny but older vehicle heading to the Garden. Pierre was a small, wiry young man with lots of energy. When he listened to boxing matches on the radio, his body mimicked every blow described by the announcers.

"We have to win tonight," said Pierre. "With that shut out in game three, we are now down 2 to 1. I'm putting my money on Sanford. He came through with two goals in the second game and away from home ice."

Paul hadn't revealed it to anyone but he was putting a wager on the Canadiens tonight and for the Stanley Cup. He was a secret admirer of the outspoken and intense Maurice Richard. While local Bruin fans were appalled at his violent style of play, Paul accepted it as the qualities of a pro. As far as Paul was concerned, no one could play right wing like the 'Rocket.'

A dejected Pierre left the Garden that night. Montreal had beaten the Bruins by a score of 7 to 3. Maurice Richard had scored three times. Unable to keep it to himself, Paul revealed, "I came out a winner. I placed my money on the Canadiens."

"You did?" questioned a surprised Pierre. "You're a turncoat."

Paul answered with an unusual swagger, "When it comes to money, you have to go with the winners. You can't let your emotions get in the way."

It was a quiet ride home. Pierre's Bruins had lost two games at home and were returning to the Forum in Montreal. Plus, he was disappointed in his brother-in-law. He hadn't seen this side of Paul in the past.

Paul in the meantime was calculating his winnings that would allow him to pay back his brother, Bill, and the amount he had secretly taken from the till. He took a deep breath. He had escaped that one. Something inside told him that he had been lucky this time. And faintly he promised himself to avoid doing it again."

Two by Each
Chapter Twenty-eight

Pierre Lepage's family had gathered around him at the small air terminal in New Bedford. Contrary to his expectations of being sent to Korea, he had received orders to report to Germany. The propeller driven aircraft on the landing strip gleamed in the sunlight. After many hugs and kisses, he joined the other passengers in the outdoor row that led to the stairway that had been moved to the side door of the aircraft. In full military uniform, he turned back to his family and friends and saluted prior to entering the plane.

When the borders between East Germany and West Berlin were closed by Russia, tensions between East and West had continued to escalate. Dwight D. Eisenhower had been elected president following Truman. Just before his election he captivated the imagination of the country by promising to go personally to Korea and end that conflict. When Joseph Stalin died a few months after taking office, Eisenhower had sought to extend an olive branch to the new Soviet regime. However, the continued turmoil in Moscow only deepened what was now being referred to as a cold war.

Pierre found his seat toward the back of the plane. The aisle sloped at an angle from front to back so that Pierre awkwardly slipped into the aisle seat.

"That was a bit of a challenge," he remarked to the gentleman beside him. Pierre offered, "I'm flying to LaGuardia and then meeting up with my platoon for a flight to Germany."

"I'm George Brown," the passenger beside him said as he introduced himself. "I make this trip to New York every couple of months. Our corporate offices are in the city. The larger planes you will be taking to Germany won't have these aisles that slope to the rear of the plane. However, unless you are flying on a commercial flight, the troop transport aircrafts don't usually provide these soft seats."

Soon after taking flight, Pierre looked across the aisle to the window and thought he saw the spire of St. Anthony's Church as the plane circled on an angle before levelling off for the remainder of the flight to New York.

"Is this your first flight?" asked Mr. Brown.

Pierre nodded, "Yes. I guess it shows." A few minutes later, he asked, "Can we smoke?"

"Absolutely! We can smoke and drink all the way. It can get a little hazy in here after a while."

Pierre didn't usually smoke too much, less than a pack a day. However, when he was nervous as he was at the moment, he could drag on a cigarette one after the other. Mr. Brown took out a pipe, filled it meticulously with a sweet smelling tobacco, and blew out circles of smoke as he lit and pulled on his pipe. Both men sat back and relaxed.

A squeaky loudspeaker broke the silence and made some announcement which Pierre could not understand. A few minutes later a young woman in a blue uniform asked if he and Mr. Brown would like a drink.

Mr. Brown quickly answered, "I'll have my usual Scotch on the rocks, Betty."

Pierre thought for a while. He was tempted to ask for a beer but thought the better of it and asked for a Coke.

Mr. Brown added, "That was quite a sendoff you had just now. It looks like either you have a large family or the entire neighborhood turned out."

Pierre answered, "Most of the group was family and a few buddies. We tend to be quite a crowd when we get together. I am the first one to fly out of New Bedford."

"I understand," said Mr. Brown, "that tension is quite volatile in Germany, especially around Berlin. Many of the East Berlin workers have been protesting their working conditions imposed upon them by the Soviet Union."

Pierre answered, "I belong to an infantry division and we are being sent to beef up the Seventh Army. I'm praying that President Eisenhower will bring stability to the region and that we can avoid armed combat. However, if we have to, our division is well trained and ready to go."

Two by Each
Chapter Twenty-nine

O'Malley met his brother-in-law, Tony DeSouza, for their traditional Saturday morning breakfast at Dillard's restaurant. Over the years, these weekly meetings of the past years had become less frequent. It had become more like a monthly get-together. Tony still ordered the customary homemade pancakes and sausage but O'Malley, who frequently complained of heartburn, avoided his favorite bacon and French toast.

"I'll have two scrambled eggs with wheat toast without butter. And I'll take cream in my coffee." Looking over to Tony, he said, "Black coffee seems to do a job on my stomach these days."

The two spent little time discussing sports that morning. The loss of the Stanley Cup to Montreal was still too fresh in their minds and a terrible disappointment. So they quickly moved to the controversial headlines of the day, Joe McCarthy.

Tony asked, "Did you know that the young Robert Kennedy has been appointed as an assistant counsel to McCarthy's Subcommittee?"

"No," answered O'Malley." "I guess I shouldn't be surprised. His father has been such a vocal anti-communist. I just hope Robert doesn't get influenced by Senator McCarthy's chief counsel, Roy Cohn. Those hearings that are on TV just turn me off. McCarthy seems to feel he is free to make any type of hostile innuendos without any evidence."

"I know what you mean," agreed Tony. "The way Voice of America personnel were questioned in front of television cameras and a packed press gallery is certainly not consistent with the Fundamentals of American Law that we studied at Boston College. It's all playing well with the television audience who fear for the safety of the country."

O'Malley added, "But it is also undermining our judicial system that supports a presumption of innocence until proven guilty for all of our citizens. We all follow rumors in our police investigations but we don't make them public or present them to the District Attorney for prosecution until we can substantiate them with facts. I'm glad to see that Father John Cronin, who has authored many anti-communist pieces, has taken exception to McCarthy's tactics."

Changing the subject, O'Malley remarked, "I understand that your wife, Dee, is joining Maria and my girls for a trip to Boston today. You should see the excitement in our house. A shopping trip to Filene's basement and a luncheon downtown is like Christmas season all over again."

"Dee was up early and dressed before I left the house," agreed Tony. "I'm quite sure they must be on the road already. Yesterday, I was worried that we might have some weather. But the sun is shining bright. I think a lot of prayers stormed heaven last night."

"Dan, have you been to a doctor lately?" asked Tony. "I don't like the way you complain about your stomach."

"It's been a few years now," answered O'Malley. "Maria has been encouraging me to make an appointment. Even though I keep most of my complaints to myself, she's picked up on my discomfort. I guess she has noticed some of the changes in my eating habits."

"You might be developing a stomach ulcer," commented Tony. "You certainly have enough stress in your job. One of our guys in the office was treated for an ulcer and seems to be doing just fine now. Before that he was constantly drinking this white chalky liquid called Maalox. It supposedly coated his stomach lining. He went to a Doctor Zipolski. I'd look him up, if I were you."

"Thanks for your interest and advice," answered O'Malley. "I promise to follow up on your recommendation of this doctor. I presume he is in the yellow pages."

"Well, I have to get going," said Tony. "Our tennis group will be waiting for me at the courts. I'm matching up with Mike Kramer. He's an old timer but is steady as a rock on the court. His play at the net continues to amaze me. Such quick reflexes."

"Dan, what are your plans for today?" Tony asked O'Malley, "now that you have the day to yourself?"

"I have a case that's been growing more complex every time new information comes forward. I'm going to take some quiet time to review the file," answered O'Malley. "Our new Chief, Guerney, is growing impatient with the lack of progress."

Two by Each
Book Seven

Two by Each
Book Seven

Chapter Thirty

Some light from the West

Inspector O'Malley's meticulous review of the Weigand case on Sunday and his meeting with Detective Barrett on Monday had proven frustrating. All leads that had been followed hadn't produced any results.

One new detail provided by Arthur Lerner that a light was on in Mr. Weigand's office, could possibly be promising.

Barrett indicated, "It could point to someone breaking into the building to steal some money which the bank president assures us was not ever present in that building. And that would point to a person totally unrelated to the affairs in the office – a total stranger. And that could be a very difficult person to find."

O'Malley picked up on that line of reasoning.

"That could possibly explain why Mr. Weigand was first found hanging from the rafters. That person could have been trying to scare Mr. Weigand into telling him where the money was. But no amount of threats could have provided that information. And it could explain the puzzling removal of the body."

"Let's put this case on the back burner for a while," said O'Malley. "We have other cases to work on."

Meanwhile, in the north end of the city Anne Lepage was reading a letter that she and Claude had received from Claude's sister, Martha. She had found the letter unopened on the front hall table when she returned home from her day of teaching. The letter expressed all kinds of excitement about coming home and seeing the family. Martha had rarely written to them over the last few years, except for Christmas. They had kept up with Martha's exploits on the West Coast through Claude's sisters who corresponded with her frequently.

When Claude came in later in time to clean up and sit down to dinner, Anne gave him Martha's letter to read. As she handed it to him, a bewildered Anne exclaimed, "Martha doesn't know that Mr. Weigand is dead and missing."

Claude read the letter carefully and said, "You're right. Toward the end of the letter she's wondering if I can arrange a meeting with her friend Mortimer whom she hasn't seen in years." He added, "I guess my sisters never mentioned it in their letters to her. They're probably more focused on sharing their love lives."

"This is going to be quite a shock to her," commented Anne. "We've been so busy with the restaurant that we never thought to make sure she had gotten the word. Little did I realize so many people ate fish and chips during Lent!"

Claude added, "Martha is already on her way home by train. There is no way we can notify her before she arrives."

Two by Each
Chapter Thirty-one

Martha Lepage and Barbara O'Toole had just boarded the California Zephyr passenger train for their four day crossing to the East Coast. They were as excited as young school girls.

Martha commented, "We haven't seen our families in such a long time. Everyone will have grown up so much since then."

"I know," answered Barbara, "my mother tells me that my brother, Sean, is over six feet tall."

The two nurses had been working at the Veterans Home in the beautiful Napa Valley. Their friendship and admiration for each other had continued to blossom from the days they had been student nurses in the White Home of St. Luke's Hospital in New Bedford.

Barbara was still petite with a delightful smile that beamed a sense of deep peace and happiness. She was still rather reserved. Martha was almost an opposite. She was vivacious and a ball of energy. Amazingly, she had to work hard at keeping her weight under control. Both were well respected nurses at the VA. Martha worked at the ER of the hospital located on the grounds while Barbara provided nursing supervision in the many cottages that dotted the beautifully landscaped campus.

A year earlier they started renting an apartment together just three bus stops away from the main gate of the Veterans Home. They had been to every wine tasting in the valley, not just once because every year new vintages were featured by the various vineyards. When their days off coincided, they were frequent visitors to downtown San Francisco. On one vacation they had travelled south to Los Angeles. The highlight of that trip was their visit to the MGM Studios lot in Beverly Hills. They had seen the famous light pole used by Gene Kelly in 'Singing in the Rain' as well as the dressing room used by his co-star Debbie Reynolds.

The train had left the Bay Area of San Francisco at exactly 10:45 a.m. and by noon time they were enjoying lunch in the dining car.

"I'll have the salmon with green beans and rice." Barbara ordered.

Martha was tempted to order the classic Amtrak burger but decided to follow Martha's lead. Four days of sitting on the train would be quite a contrast from her long walks around the extended campus of the VA. Looking up at the waiter dressed in a well-tailored black suit with a white towel over his left forearm, she ordered.

"I'll also have the salmon but with asparagus and a baked potato."

"And what would the ladies wish to drink?" asked the waiter. "We serve a nice delicate Merlot from the Beaulieu Vineyards."

Both women looked at each other and said almost in unison, "Why not, we're going home."

Barbara commented, "Have you ever seen so much clean white linen? And look at all the glassware."

Martha added, "And the utensils are all shiny silverware and even the tops of the salt and pepper shakers are sparkling."

When the waiter returned with their luncheon meal, he pointed out the window. "We are leaving our state capital.

Sacramento is a delightful place to visit. One of my brothers lives there and I visit with him and his family as often as I can."

While they ate lunch, and then later seated in the vista dome observation car, both were awed by the breathtaking views before them. The peaks of the Sierra Nevada Mountains were still covered with snow. They overheard a woman who had a brochure in her hands,

"We are heading through Donner Pass."

As they came through the Pass, a large lake opened up before them on their side of the train.

Martha exclaimed, "Look how the sun is playing on the lake and the hills in the background as it peeks in and out of the clouds."

When the sun finally set behind the moving train and another scrumptious meal had been eaten, Martha and Barbara retired to their sleeper. The room was small and cozy and again everything was extremely clean and tidy. It wasn't long before they fell asleep. The motion of the train beneath them and sharing another bottle of wine had been better than any sleeping aid.

Throughout the night they had travelled through Nevada. At breakfast they were told that before noon they would arrive at Salt Lake City.

"The train will be stopping over for two hours and passengers can leave the train. We'll be cleaning up here and bringing on fresh provisions and a Helper engine is attached for the trip through the Colorado Rockies. There's time to visit the Mormon Tabernacle on Temple Square. You won't be able to visit the Mormon Temple itself. That building is closed to the public. However, the huge Tabernacle is open. Most days someone is playing on the organ which has more than a ten thousand pipes. The acoustics are remarkable. I would recommend it." The waiter informed them.

By two o'clock the Zephyr was heading to the Colorado border. The scenery on the eastern edge of Utah began to change quickly as the Rocky Mountains beckoned them forward. Once the train reached Grand Junction the train snaked for hours through majestic canyons.

Martha pointed out to Barbara, "We can see the front of the train as it semi-circles around that mountainside."

Not long afterwards the conductor announced to the passengers.

"We have reached our highest elevation. We are at 9,200 feet above sea level. Soon we will enter the Moffat Tunnel which is over 6 miles long. The tunnel opened in 1928. It shaves 176 miles off our journey."

When they came back out into daylight Barbara was ecstatic.

"It's just so beautiful. With the sun edging over the mountains behind us, the shadows give us a better appreciation of the depths below us and the heights of the mountain ranges."

Before nightfall, the Zephyr had descended to the mile high city of Denver. The train stopped for only a half hour for refueling and servicing at Denver's historic Union Station. Martha and Barbara had decided to have their dinner at the last seating. They had been too busy viewing the splendor of the mountains. As they slept that night the Zephyr continued its journey through Nebraska and Iowa. They were having breakfast when they were told that they were crossing the Mississippi River. In a few hours, they had arrived in Chicago where they later embarked on the 20th Century Limited for the final leg of their journey to Grand Central Terminal in New York City.

With the repetitive views of corn fields and silos outside the train windows, Martha began to share with Barbara the concern she had for Mortimer Weigand. Barbara had been made aware of the nursing care that Martha provided to Mortimer many years earlier when he arrived from the Pacific. He had sustained serious injuries when his ship had been sunk by the Japanese. Shrapnel in his spine had left him partially paralyzed, and a broken depressed man. With her nursing care and a growing friendship, Mortimer had undergone a successful surgery that had removed the shrapnel and left him with only a slight limp due to some nerve damage.

Martha told Barbara. "A few months ago and out of the blue, Mortimer wrote to me. It was a strange letter. He indicated that he was going through some difficult times. He expressed how important my friendship with him had been in those difficult days. He also wrote about his earlier relationship with a Maureen Moriarity. She was the daughter of his mother's housekeeper while growing up in New Bedford. With her enthusiasm and fondness for horses, she had helped him put behind the feeling of rejection he had sensed from his father. Sometimes, I felt the two of us, Maureen and me, blended into the same person."

Barbara answered, "I remember you mentioning him when I first joined you in California. The little you told me about him gave me the impression that he was a bit of a strange man."

"What worries me," continued Martha, "is that in the closing part of his rather rambling letter, he made it a point of reassuring me that everything would be fine. And not to be concerned about events in his life that I might learn about him. It ended rather abruptly, 'Thank you for your love - a friend.'"

"What are you thinking?" asked Barbara. "Do you think he is experiencing some of that dark cynicism that comes back to haunt so many of our veterans?"

"Something like that," answered Martha. "My brother, Claude, who has been working as Mortimer's chauffeur, has assured me that Mortimer is a successful business man. However, we know that even some veterans who have established prosperous careers can fall apart. After their dreadful experiences in the war, what for most people seems a normal life suddenly seems wholly and disturbingly ridiculous to them. I'm worried about him."

Two by Each
Chapter Thirty-two

On the Friday before Easter two young women were paying their cab fare in front of the Lepage three decker in New Bedford. After reaching their destination in New York City, they had taken a train to Providence. Martha had been informed in the many letters she had received from her family that almost everyone was pitching in to help their brother, Claude, in his fish and chip restaurant. The Fridays in Lent had been especially busy and Good Friday would finally wrap things up.

Mrs. Lepage was the only one at home when Martha knocked at the rear door of the family tenement. Martha's mother animatedly welcomed her daughter and her companion Barbara.

"I've been waiting here all nervous and excited," she said as she hugged her Martha and Barbara into a wide and warm embrace. "Come, bring in your bags. The boys have vacated their room for you. They plan to sleep on the couches in the front parlor."

There was a light lunch where endless and enthusiastic descriptions of the trip across country were related.

Mrs. Lepage informed her guests, "I was planning to attend the Good Friday services. Do you want to join me? Everyone else in the family is busy. It's so different from the days when you were a young girl, Martha. It seemed then that everything just stood still for three hours."

Barbara and Martha had been faithful church goers during their years on the West Coast. They had participated not only in Catholic services at the chapel on the VA grounds but had attended ceremonies of worship of the many other denominations offered for the residents.

Together they walked the few blocks to St. Joseph's Church. As they climbed up the stairs to the large front doors, Martha's mind was filled with the many memories of her childhood. Where Martha's mother had once held her hand to assist her up the stairs, now she and Barbara were assisting her mother to climb the stairs.

"These knees are getting quite stiff," Mrs. Lepage commented with a smile.

Glancing at Barbara, Martha explained, "She's washed too many floors on her knees."

"And I'm sure your mother spent many hours on her knees praying for your large family," added Barbara.

As they entered the vestibule of the church, a reverential quiet and silence overtook them. The smell of incense used in the Holy Thursday celebrations still filled the air. The church was more than half-filled with most of the front pews filled with fidgeting children who attended the parochial school next door. The Sisters in their black habits and starched white bibs were closely observing their charges. As they stood at the end of the aisles, their eyes spoke volumes to those who might poke a neighbor or dare to giggle.

The elderly Monsignor entered the sanctuary and took a seat in the large chair that would allow him to preside over the afternoon service. One of the younger parish priests, accompanied by a large retinue of altar boys, started the solemn Way of the Cross. Barbara hadn't anticipated that the prayers at each station would be all in French, while the hymns sung as they marched from one station to the other were in Latin.

Martha found herself being distracted as she looked over the rows of school children some pews in front of her. She thought she recognized the hairdo of Charlotte, her niece. She was now in the eighth grade and would be graduating soon. She kept looking for Louise and Andrew but the taller eighth graders hid the smaller school children from her view. So much had happened in the last three years since her last visit home. Her sister, Claudia, had a little girl of her own. Another sister had married, and her brother, Pierre, was in the army serving in Germany.

When they returned home after the church services, Mrs. Lepage informed Martha and Barbara, "We have to get ready for the little ones. Al and Janet are busy on Friday evening helping at the restaurant. When Andrew comes rushing in, he is always famished and looks forward to one of Memere's surprises."

Sure enough, not long afterwards, three excited young people came rushing up the back porch stairway and rushed into the rear hallway to the back door. Andrew had pushed his way to the front. Charlotte had turned up her eyes and just looked at him with disgust. He was so immature.

Charlotte held back and let her younger siblings overwhelm their aunt, Martha. She introduced herself to Barbara.

"You are as pretty as you are in the photos that Aunt Martha has sent us."

And Barbara commented, "And you have become quite the sophisticated young lady. I love what you have done with your hair."

Only Martha's father and one of her brothers, Jean Paul, joined them for supper that night. The social club where her father tended bar had closed in order to observe the solemnity of Good Friday.

He explained, "We spent the day cleaning the club. It's not very often that the place is empty. Then we had to set tables for a party celebration on Easter Sunday. The large Poyant family is gathering from all over. You'll remember, Martha, that's where we bought our shoes at their store on the Avenue."

The remainder of the evening was hectic. First Al and Janet came home from the restaurant. Exchanges were somewhat brief as Al had to be up early the next morning and Andrew, especially, needed to be washed and ready for bed. Janet had agreed that Charlotte could stay and visit with her aunt. Louise was disappointed and reluctantly walked up the stairs to the third floor tenement. Later Martha's two sisters who still lived at home arrived. The group of women ventured into the front parlor and excited conversations could be heard throughout the house. Mr. Lepage settled in his chair to read the newspaper.

Jean Paul found a comic book and started to read but eventually announced to his father, "I'm going for a walk. There's just too much noise around here."

Two by Each
Chapter Thirty-three

Before noon the following day, Martha was driving to Taunton where Barbara would be celebrating Easter with her family. She borrowed the family Chevy Coupe after dropping off her father at the social club. She arranged to pick him up by nine o'clock that evening. Her brother, Jean Paul, had expressed a lot of concern about her borrowing the family vehicle. He had contributed heavily on this family purchase. From his salary working steadily as a carpenter, he had made the down payment and paid about half of the monthly payments of $26.70 on the loan. In his estimation he considered it his own car and spent considerable time cleaning and polishing it.

Mr. O'Toole welcomed his daughter, Barbara, with the biggest smile and at first extended his hand to Martha but quickly changed his mind and grabbed her in his arms. Martha had only met him once and that was at the graduation ceremony from the St. Luke's Nursing School.

He had a strong Irish accent and looking at Martha, said, "Welcome to our home. Mrs. O'Toole won't be home 'til much later. Today is one of the busiest days at the hat shop on the Green. Women and girls are picking up their fancy bonnets for Easter Sunday."

Barbara added, "There's a lot of last minute fitting and adjustments to be made. My mother just loves that part of her job and all the proud poses she observes as the shoppers glance at themselves in the mirror."

Barbara brought her luggage to her old room where she showed Martha some of her childhood items that her mother had displayed on her bureau and nightstand. Barbara pointed out one photo.

"That picture was taken at my first communion. I just loved that white dress. I think that's when I first decided on becoming a nurse. One of my mother's sisters is a nurse and I just admired her white uniform."

Mr. O'Toole called out, "Tea is ready."

"Your mother made some of your favorite biscuits. And she gave me another series of instructions on how to steep the tea before serving. As if I would forget!" He pointed out, as they entered the kitchen.

Barbara sensed that her father was a bit restless as they sipped tea and daintily ate biscuits. They were reminiscing and sharing some of their experiences of their cross country trip, when suddenly her father blurted out, "Do you want to see Molly, our cow?" Since her last visit home, Mr. O'Toole had purchased a milking cow from one of his neighbors.

Mr. O'Toole slipped on a pair of rubber boots. "Just be careful where you step," he advised. "I cleaned up the area this morning in anticipation of your visit." As they approached the new barn that had been built adjacent to the small family vegetable garden, they could see a rather large cow laying down chewing her cud on a muddy area of her enclosure.

Both young ladies looked at each other with a certain distress, Barbara stating, "And to think we drink the milk that comes from such a dirty old cow."

Barbara's father clarified, "I clean Molly's udder thoroughly before milking her and then one of the neighbors who also has a dairy pasteurizes the milk before we drink it."

Martha added, "My father once owned a dairy but lost it during the Depression. I was too young to remember it."

Mr. O'Toole continued, "I find caring for Molly and working with your mother in the garden so invigorating and relaxing." Looking at Martha, he explained, "My days at the factory working as a silversmith are creative but also very tedious. These outdoor activities are so refreshing – a chance to use my muscles not just my eyes and hands. The best part about caring for Molly is that it is a year around job not just in the summer months. I think I especially like it in the winter time when I have to trudge over to the barn in the early morning to milk her and set her up for the day before I leave for work. Even shoveling snow to get to the barn doesn't seem as strenuous as clearing the snow away from the path that leads to the driveway and the mail box on the side of the road."

Two by Each
Chapter Thirty-four

Later that evening, Martha joined Claude and Anne in the apartment that they shared with Anne's parents. The Saulniers had gone to visit a sick relative at St. Luke's Hospital and to dinner at a local restaurant. It was a Saturday night tradition, plus it would allow their daughter, Anne, some private time with Claude. This particular night Claude especially appreciated it. He had been uncertain on how to break the news about Mortimer's death to his sister Martha.

Martha had been a bit surprised by the lingering odor of fried food that filled the apartment. Anne explained, "The clothes we wore at the restaurant have been stored away in the rear entry. We have become almost immune to it. I even put on a little extra of my best perfume to cover it over for you."

Mrs. Saulnier had prepared a meat pie for them to share. Claude noticed that, after three long days behind the fry-o-lators, he would lose his appetite. He enjoyed a cold beer with a small slice of the meat pie covered with his mother-in-law's delicious brown gravy. Anne and Martha joined him but with a glass of iced tea. The Lenten season, with its days of fasting and abstinence, was over. Martha welcomed a second piece of meat pie. It had been years since she had enjoyed the French Canadian treat.

As Anne was clearing away the table, Claude commented, "We have apple pie for dessert. Since you've been away Al has started selling Brenneke's pies. They are the best. They have a real light crust and in season their blueberry pie is fabulous."

Claude finally approached the delicate subject of Mortimer's death. The issue had been a cloud hanging over him.

He started, "You asked me about arranging a meeting with Mortimer." At this Martha's eyes brightened. "However, I'm afraid that is not possible." Martha forehead wrinkled with a frown, and asked, "Why not? Is he away?"

"In a way, you could say that," he answered. Claude described how he had discovered Mortimer's body without any of the details and how it was missing when he later returned with the police.

Martha sat there absolutely stunned. Anne reached over and held her hand. "When did this happen?" Martha asked. "I received a letter from him not that long ago."

Martha suddenly rose from her chair at the dining room table and picked up her purse from the chair nearby. "Look, here is the letter. I was looking forward to sharing it with you. There's a part of his letter that is rather strange and I thought you might shed some light on it. But I never expected this." She handed the letter over to Claude. He took the letter out of the envelope and read it carefully, going over certain sections more than once.

Claude passed the letter to Anne and scratching his head asked, "When did you receive this letter?"

"I don't remember exactly when but it was some time ago now," Martha answered.

In turn Martha enquiringly asked, "When did you discover Mortimer's body?"

Claude answered, "It was before we bought the restaurant which was a few weeks before Ash Wednesday. We only had a short time to get ready for the busy season. Mrs. Moriarity and I were kept on to watch his house in New Bedford for about a month. A few weeks later Al informed me of the upcoming sale of the fish and chip store. I would say about three months ago."

Anne stood up from her chair and said, "Just a second. I can tell you the exact date."

When she returned from the bedroom she shared with Claude, she had a small calendar in her hands. Looking over to Martha, Anne explained, "I had a miscarriage a few days before Claude's discovery. It was a Monday morning and Claude had accompanied me on my way to school that morning." Glancing affectionately at Claude, she continued, "Your brother is such a dear."

"My sisters had written to me about your loss, Anne," she stated. "I didn't know how to approach this subject with the two of you, so I didn't even write to you about it. I'm so sorry."

"Here it is," Anne pointed out on the calendar. "Claude walked me to Normandin on Monday, January 18th, and later that morning he discovered Mortimer's body."

Anne reached for the letter that was on the table. She searched to see if Mortimer had dated it, but didn't find such an entry at the top of the letter. "Can I see the envelope?" asked Anne. Martha handed it to her. To her surprise, she read aloud, "This letter was stamped on January 24th. There is no return address or post office marking. Is it possible that Mortimer is still alive?"

"Oh, my God!" exclaimed Martha. "What is this all about?"

Two by Each

Book Eight

Two by Each
Book Eight

Chapter Thirty-five

Going forward

On Monday afternoon Martha Lepage accompanied her brother, Claude, to a meeting with Chief Inspector Daniel O'Malley. Anne had insisted that this new information be shared with the police. The inspector welcomed them warmly and introduced, "This is Inspector Joseph Barrett. He's has been the lead investigator on the Mortimer Weigand case."

The Inspector apologized for receiving them in a rather sterile interview room, "Please, don't let the atmosphere of this room distress you," he started. "It was the only room available on short notice."

O'Malley sat across the table from the Lepages and the inspector stood to the side. "Your brother informed me on the telephone this morning that you had brought some surprising material with you from the West Coast. Then together you had made an astonishing and rather disquieting discovery in reference to Mr. Weigand's disappearance."

Martha reached into her purse and retrieved the letter that she had received from Mortimer Weigand.

"I received this letter from Mortimer a while ago," she started. "It was a bit mysterious but in some way not unlike the Mortimer I had gotten to know while he convalesced at the Oakland Naval Hospital. I had been assigned to assist him in finding the mental courage to undergo surgery that promised to relieve his pain and restore his ability to walk. He had become terribly depressed. This condition, I was to learn, had been part of his life as a youth. A young girl, Maureen Moriarity, who was part of the family household, had helped him through this difficult and dark period."

Martha continued, "The last time I saw Mortimer was at his mother's funeral. I was home on leave at the time. For a period of time we corresponded and then it ended. And then I received this quite unexpected letter."

Inspector O'Malley read the letter aloud so that Detective Barrett could hear it as well. "It is a bit strange. However, your brother told me that it led you to some unexpected discovery."

Claude answered, "If you look at the date stamp on the envelope, you will see that it was stamped about a week after I made my discovery of him hanging in his office."

Inspector O'Malley opened a file that lay on the table before him. Upon consulting it, he looked over to Detective Barrett, "Claude reported his discovery on Monday, January 18th, and this letter was post marked on January 24th."

Martha continued, "The more I thought about this inconsistency, as I lay awake last night, I believe I may have found an answer to this puzzle. The psychiatrists at the hospital in Oakland had diagnosed Mortimer as manic-depressive. Not only did he suffer from serious bouts of depression but in contrast he would occasionally exhibit some extreme manic behaviors. He would easily become overexcited or agitated as well as hyperactive. This manic phase is what I detect in his letter. For reasons I do not even venture to guess, Mortimer may have staged his own death and went into hiding. But he couldn't keep this to himself, and so the reason for this letter."

Detective Joseph Barrett, who had stood silent near the table, approached a few steps and reflected, "That is very enlightening information you are providing. Your conclusions bring a whole different dimension to this case."

O'Malley agreed, "There was always a slight probability that Mr. Weigand might have survived the hanging. However, Claude, your description of what you saw as you entered the second floor office, especially the black tongue protruding from his mouth and that his hands were tied behind his back, disproved any possibility of it being self-inflicted. Your description led to a conclusion that it was either an execution or a threat gone badly."

Joe Barrett continued, "Claude, Mr. Weigand could have reasonably presumed that you would come looking for him that morning. The staging of the hanging is quite elaborate but would be in keeping with your sister's knowledge of his mental condition."

Inspector O'Malley thanked the Lepages for the information that they had brought to bear on their investigation. "Please," he concluded, "share any other information that may come to mind and especially if Mr. Weigand attempts to contact either one of you. Of course, there is the probability that the letter was written prior to his death and given to someone else and mailed later. However, I agree with you, Ms. Lepage, that the letter seems to refer to the incident that your brother discovered."

After the Lepages departed the police station, Inspector O'Malley and detective Joe Barrett consulted together in O'Malley's office. O'Malley started, "As intriguing as the assumptions and conclusions provided to us by Ms. Lepage, we have only the concrete evidence that a letter was mailed and post marked one week after the discovery by her brother of Mortimer hanging in his office on the waterfront."

Two by Each
Chapter Thirty-six

Jean Paul had finished his day's work on the construction of a new home in the far north end of the city. His co-worker, John Desautel, had picked him up at 5:30 earlier that morning on the avenue up the street from where he lived. He was dressed in his bib overalls. The day was promising to be warm so he had put on a lighter work shirt than the plaid broadcloth woolen one he had been wearing the past months. He carried a black lunch box that held two thick sandwiches his mother had made for him, plus an apple that she insisted he bring along with him. A Thermos of lemonade with a few chips of ice was held safely in the inside rounded cover by a clip.

The work day on the construction sites normally ended by 3:00 but this day they had remained on the job just beyond four o'clock. Jean Paul and John were laying a new wooden floor in the front room and Mr. Domingos Medeiros, their boss, had told them to complete the job before leaving the site.

As they were laying the tongue and groove red oak boards, Jean Paul blurted out, "Of all the days to keep us on the job. I've made arrangements to use the family car tonight. I'm picking up a friend and we are going to the Seekonk Speedway. "Radical" Rick Martin from Westport is racing tonight. Are you interested in coming? I'm picking up my friend, Jim Bergeron, at the new Orchid Diner on the corner of Kempton Street and Rockdale Avenue at six."

John answered, "My life is quite different now that I've gotten married. I can't make those kinds of impulsive choices anymore. I have to check in with Lorraine first so as to make sure we have nothing going on tonight. Plus we are starting to save any extra money. Just keep it between us for now, but Lorraine thinks that she may be pregnant. I can't believe that I may be a father in less than a year."

After cleaning up quickly and washing his hair in the bathroom sink and wiping it dry with many strokes of his towel, Jean Paul added a heavy amount of pomade to his hair. He used a heavy comb that straightened out some of his natural curls. Checking himself in the bathroom mirror countless times, Jean Paul approved the look. The pomade had darkened the natural coloring of his hair and gave it an almost black sheen.

He grabbed the keys of the family car that hung on a hook near the rear entrance of the family tenement. He rushed to his mother who was working in the small kitchen pantry and gave her a kiss on the cheek. She looked up and said, "You need a haircut, Jean Paul. And with all that goo on your hair, how can you stand it? Have a good time but be safe. Don't drive too fast, and get home early enough, so that you can get a few hours of sleep before you get up for work tomorrow. I'll put some strong coffee in your thermos instead of a cold drink."

Before getting behind the wheel of the car, Jean Paul opened the trunk and pulled out a clean rag he always kept there. He examined the exterior of the car and buffed out a few hand prints on the right mud guard. When he sighted some debris that had been left on the floor of the rear of the car, he quickly snapped it up and placed it in the trash barrel just off the rear steps of the house. He also carefully replaced the cover of the trash barrel. Jean Paul had always been neat about his appearance and the section of the bedroom he had shared with his brothers. However, his work as a finished carpenter had taught him the importance of being precise in his measurements and in the planning of the details of his project. He had learned this important part of his trade from Joao Pimentel. Jean

Paul had assisted Mr. Pimentel on the very first day on his job with the Medeiros Construction Company. Jean Paul always looked forward to being at the same work site as Mr. Pimentel. He liked to consult with him about particular details of a project that had been given to him and almost without fail; Mr. Pimentel would show him a simpler and more precise way of tackling the assignment.

Jim Bergeron was waiting on the sidewalk in front of the Orchid Diner. As he jumped into the front seat of the car, he stated, "I thought you were picking me up at five." Jean Paul explained the reason for the delay and said, "You keep an eye out for any police cars that may be in hiding behind bushes waiting to flag us down. We have some time to make up if we are going to be there in time for at least the second race."

It was a straight run up Route 6 through Dartmouth and Westport that had a four lane divided highway. The tracks of the trolleys that ran from New Bedford to Fall River could still be seen in some places of the center strip. "Getting through Fall River," stated Jean Paul, "will be the challenge." Jim suggested, "It may not be quite so bad. Most of the mill workers will be home having their suppers by now."

Except for a small delay waiting for the drawbridge to close on the Brightman Street Bridge that spanned the Taunton River between the city of Fall River and the town of Somerset, the trip to Seekonk took a little over an hour. Jim was all excited as they waited in line to pay for parking, "I think the announcer tonight is Anthony Venditti himself, the owner." When paying for parking, Jean Paul had learned that the first race had just ended.

They had to park quite a distance from the entrance of the track but the young men walked quickly through the dusty parking lot to get their entry ticket at the gate. Jim spotted a few empty seats to his right around the tenth row, "What about those seats?" he asked

Jean Paul. Jean Paul nodded and was quite surprised that such good seats might be available. He soon learned that a week earlier a tire on one of the racing cars had come crashing into the stands. The entire one third of a mile track was encircled with a tall metal chain link fence except for this spot. This was adjacent to where the stock cars entered onto the track.

Jean Paul was especially interested in the races that featured Rick Martin. He was informed that "Radical" Rick had already won the first race. He was also told that Rick was also racing in the third and fifth race. After the second race, Jim asked Jean Paul, if he wanted to put a bet on the next race?" Jean Paul nodded. OK Thinking it was a bet between the two of them; he put his hand into the pocket of his jacket and pulled out a few bills. Jim pushed Jean Paul's hand aside and said, "Come, follow me."

In whispers Jim told Jean Paul, "My uncle showed me how to make a wager at the track. It's illegal but it's done all the time." When they reached the area under the seating platform, Jim pointed out, "Each section of the track has a number. Closest to the track is number one. Look for the number painted on the steel pole. As you move to the right, the next section is two and so on. Depending on where the bookie is standing, that's the odds they are willing to pay. Every wager is on the nose and for a win, no place or show as at the dogs tracks pari-mutuel windows that are licensed by the State.

Jean Paul inquired, "How do you pick out the bookie?"

"They all wear a fedora and off to the right. Usually, they are reading a newspaper facing away from the track. There's one who is keeping an eye out for the coppers and has already spotted us as potential customers. When he turns back toward the track, he's ready to do business. You always approach him from his left and leave to the right. One avoids making a line. As they moved along the bookie closed his newspaper and turned toward the stands. Sure enough a man lingering in the area approached him from his left. In a second he had moved on.

Jim pointed out, "You'll notice that he is standing between section two and three. That means he is willing to pay two and half to one. The first four sections only accept two dollar wagers. Bookies under sections five through ten will take larger amounts from five to twenty dollars. Not too many go that far out and spend that kind of money. Just watch me."

"Oh," announced Jim, "we'll have to wait. He's turning around. He's a little uncertain as to whether he wants to do business with us. He saw all the talking we were doing. We can't approach him together. Go back toward the entrance and I'll catch up with you." Very soon Jim was by Jean Paul's side re-entering the seating area. As they sat awaiting the start of the third race, Jim flashed a small red paper cupped in his left hand. It had a 3/5 written on it. "It's our ticket for the third race and number five is the number on Rick's stock car with a brand new engine." Both had put in a dollar.

Jean Paul said, "I feel lucky."

Seven cars lined up for the third race. All had done a turn around the track testing their engines and steering. Finally the moment had arrived; the green flag at the starting line was waved high in the air. Jean Paul could hear the roar of the engines just before they passed before them on the straight away. Everyone was standing to see the flurry of cars and smoke as the cars made their way to the first banked turn on the oval track. As they crossed into view on the far side three cars were abreast with the other four trailing closely behind. Jim shouted, "I don't see number 5. Rick must be in the middle of the lead pack. Look he's moving ahead and sliding down to the inside lane as they make the far turn." Sure enough, Rick Martin was in the lead as he passed the stands.

"Two more laps to go," said Jim over the din of the crowd and with his fingers crossed. Jean Paul just stood in amazement. On the straight away on the far side, Rick's number 5 held the lead with numbers 3 and 7 stretched out behind him. Three cars were bunched up together some distance behind and number 1 was bringing up the rear with heavy smoke coming from one of the wheels.

By the time the cars came by the stands, number 7 had moved into second place. This time it was Jean Paul who shouted, "One more to go!" Again as the cars passed on the far side of the track, Rick's number 5 was still in the lead but number 7 had edged up beside him on the right as they entered the final turns.

Jim asked one of the men sitting beside him, "Do you know who is number 7?"

"It's "Crazy" Doug Bouchard from Brockton," he answered.

"Oh, boy," exclaimed Jim. This time he uncrossed his fingers and put them together in a plea of prayer. As they glanced to their left, they could see that Bouchard had come out of the turn slightly ahead of Rick Martin. On the straight away in front of them both cars were now neck in neck. The chequered flag came out and the waving signaled the official finish of the race.

"Who won?" asked Jean Paul.

"I don't know. It could be a dead heat. We'll have to wait for the officials to announce the results."

Everyone in the stands kept standing. After what seemed like forever, Anthony Venditti finally made the announcement declaring Bouchard the winner. "Two of the three officials have declared Ken Bouchard the winner over Rick Martin," Venditti calmly said over the microphone knowing that there would be lots of controversy over the call. He didn't want to add to the furor.

"Wow, that was close," said Jean Paul. "I don't know if I can take any more of this."

Jim insisted, "We have to stay for the fifth race. We'll double our bet and have another chance to win back our money with another bet on Rick Martin."

Jean Paul dug into his pocket and only came up with his last dollar bill. "That's all I have left," he explained.

"I'll cover you," said Jim. "If we win, you can pay me back from the winnings. If we lose, you can treat me to a beer next Friday night at the cock fight at the farm in Rochester."

Jean Paul replied, "I'll be happy to treat you to a beer but not at a cock fight. I found that the event totally disgusted me. There was such violence and blood. It makes me sick to just think of it. I don't see any fun in putting innocent animals through it and then betting on it."

Jim encouraged Jean Paul to make the wager for the fifth race. They spotted the bookie directly under the fourth section. "The odds are in our favor," declared Jim. Jean Paul did the quick transaction and showed the 5/5 small card to Jim as they got back to their seats. The fifth race turned out to be anti-climactic. Rick Martin led the field and took the chequered flag speeding away. As Martin was taking a victory lap with the chequered flag, Jim and Jean Paul were already collecting their sixteen dollar winnings.

On the way home, Jean Paul mentioned, "When I was waiting to lay the wager for the fifth race, I could have sworn that I recognized the person who approached the bookie ahead of me. I'm almost sure it was the guy my brother worked for as his chauffeur. The strange thing is that this man is supposed to be dead. Although it is true they never found his body."

"Are you sure?" questioned Jim.

"I'm pretty sure," answered Jean Paul. "I did some carpentry work for him at his home on Mechanics Lane in New Bedford. The kitchen windows and the rear door of the old house needed to be repaired. I worked there for three Saturdays about a year ago. He would usually be home on Saturday mornings and would come to supervise my work. He was tall and had a limp."

"Did this guy have a limp?" asked Jim.

"I didn't notice," answered Jean Paul.

Two by Each
Chapter Thirty-seven

Inspector O'Malley was sitting in the office of FBI Agent William Normandin in the federal building in Boston. This was his first visit to the FBI office of his former detective. O'Malley took a special pride in the accomplishments of his protégé in whom he had detected great promise many years earlier. Bill Normandin had been assigned to a case when he was in his first year as a policeman walking a beat in the French Canadian section of the city. Even as a young man, Bill knew his people and how to handle them. He also exhibited an uncanny ability to analyze a lot of details and uncover common threads that helped unravel cases.

However, Daniel O'Malley was not in Boston just to exchange pleasantries and take a walk down memory lane. When O'Malley had shared the letter that Ms. Martha Lepage received from Mr. Weigand, the Chief insisted that O'Malley personally approach the FBI and get the facts. The Chief insisted, "The FBI knows a hell of a lot more about this case than they have so far shared with us. Get to the bottom of this and soon before the press make us into a laughing stock. Take advantage of your previous connection with the agent in charge."

As he was about to leave his office for the drive to Boston, O'Malley had received a call from Claude Lepage. He told O'Malley that my brother Jean Paul told me that he thinks he saw Mr. Mortimer Weigand at the Seekonk Raceway a few nights ago.

O'Malley related how angered and dissatisfied his chief was with the information the New Bedford Police Department had so far received from the FBI on this joint case. Without revealing his hand regarding the recent information he had received from the Lepages, the inspector asked, "What can I bring back to my boss? I don't want just the few names of Mr. Weigand's local contacts and a sketchy description of his clandestine operation. The Chief wants to be on the inside tract so that he won't be blindsided. Bill, I need details."

Bill Normandin had seen this side of the inspector on only a few occasions in the past and it brought back memories of their work together. O'Malley in most instances was somewhat laid back and let his detectives pursue a case at their own speed. However, in certain circumstances O'Malley could be a real bull dog. This was one of those times.

Agent Normandin stood up from his desk and took a seat in the chair near Inspector O'Malley on the same side of the desk. "This is off the records," he said. "I will leave it to your best judgment as to what you bring back to your Chief. Knowing you, all this information will be shared with him even the nuances. By the way, that's the way I work with my director. Not all agents follow this code. We are given a lot of latitude in our cases, especially with our undercover contacts."

"Let me start from the beginning," said Normandin. "As I told you previously, we had recruited Mr. Weigand as part of what is now named 'Operation Washtub.' It started out as a concern for intrusion into Alaska by Communist Russia, and expanded to the East Coast. Because of his distinguished service in the Navy during the War and his experience with the New Bedford fishing operations, it was decided that he was an excellent candidate to fill this position. He recruited small time fishermen, helped them update their radio equipment and assigned them areas of the coast to patrol. The work he was doing of keeping track of the fishing fleet for Mr. Willard at the bank provided a perfect cover for this part of the operation."

O'Malley interjected, "What can you add to these details that have already been shared with us?"

"I was coming to that," answered Normandin. "Sometime before the incident you uncovered at Mr. Weigand's office that early Monday morning, Mortimer informed me that he suspected that his cover had been blown. He even thought that his life might be in danger. He never did explain to me where that threat on his life might be coming from. Knowing something of his prior mental state from that case that you and I had investigated together in New Bedford, I even wondered whether he was experiencing a meltdown – some kind of paranoia. That's why we approached you when we learned of his being found hanged in his office and that his body subsequently disappeared. We first learned of that from the press. That didn't sit well with my director. We weren't sure as to whether we were up against a major threat to our entire operation or if I had a rogue operative in my unit."

"I can tell you that we have had no subsequent contact with Lieutenant Weigand," continued Agent Normandin. "He has just faded into thin air."

Inspector O'Malley then related, "In the last few days we have come across some rather startling discoveries. One was a letter from him that was mailed a week after the office incident. I was just told this morning that someone thought they spotted Mortimer Weigand at a public event about an hour's drive from New Bedford."

Bill Normandin's eyes opened wide in disbelief but he was also extremely grateful for this new information. O'Malley further explained the details of these breakthroughs and the role that the members of the Lepage family had played in them.

Bill ventured, "I suspect that if Mortimer Weigand is reluctant to contact me directly, it probably suggests to him that the leak in his operation is internal."

O'Malley countered, "There is a slight chance that he may contact Martha Lepage again."

Bill Normandin reacted, "That would be a best scenario. He trusts her. She could become our go between."

"In the meantime," continued O'Malley, "I think we need to investigate the money side. He needs to be supporting himself somehow. There must be a trail."

Normandin agreed, "He had been receiving some financial support from us. I'll check that out."

O'Malley suggested, "I'll check with Mr. Willard. He has control of the family trust. He could also have knowledge of other accounts directly in Mortimer's name."

Two by Each
Chapter Thirty-eight

When Inspector O'Malley walked up the front steps to his single family home in the city's west end, his daughter Margaret greeted him at the door. He had observed her peeking through the sheer curtains in the front room. When he saw the expression on her face, he immediately concluded that something was wrong. "What is the matter, Margaret?" he asked.

Holding back some tears and a lump in her throat, Margaret struggled to answer, "Vavó has been rushed to the hospital. She burned herself on the stove. Uncle Tony picked up Mommy a little while ago and they have gone to see her. She asked that you meet them there. I'm waiting for Julia to get home. She's practicing for the end of the school year musical. When she gets home, we'll say the rosary together waiting for you to return from the hospital."

O'Malley found his brother in law, Tony, in the waiting room of the emergency area of St. Luke's Hospital. After a light handshake and a stronger hug, Tony informed Danny, "Maria and my sister, Melissa, are with my mother. They are limiting the number of visitors. My wife just came down from the floor where she was working. As a nurse she felt that she would have no trouble joining them."

"I'm so sorry," stated O'Malley. "Do you know what happened?"

"Not much," Tony answered. "I was still at work when my sister Melissa called me and told me that my mother was at the stove preparing something when one of her sleeves caught fire. Melissa was home at the time. Fortunately, she has Thursday off. She was upstairs in her room, and began to smell smoke. She found my mother at the sink running water over her arm. It was pretty bad, and Melissa told me that the right side of her face was all blistered."

The two men eventually sat down. But in a few minutes, Tony was up. He said, "I just can't sit there. I have to walk around."

After what seemed to be an interminable wait, Tony saw his wife Deolinda coming through the doors of the emergency area. Tony hastily went over to meet her. Danny slowly reached them, hanging back a bit to allow Tony and Deo time together. When Deo saw Danny, she brought him into their conversation. She was reassuring Tony.

"Your mother will recover. It may take some time. She has sustained some serious burns on her arm. The doctor treating her indicates that the majority of the burns are first or second degree. They've penetrated the epidermis and the layer of the skin beneath it. These are intensely painful as your mother's face exhibits. With proper care these will heal and leave no scarring. However, the doctor's major concern is an area near your mother's right elbow. Your mother doesn't seem to feel much discomfort there and that's the trouble. It points to nerve damage and a deeper third degree burn. Her face looks terrible but these in fact are minor burns. These should heal in a week or so."

Sometime later Maria Fatima DeSouza was admitted to a room in the hospital. All gathered around her. After a while Deo said, "The medication is starting to make her sleepy. It's best we let her rest. I'll come back to see her after I end my shift. If I don't call you tonight, it will mean nothing has changed for the worse. I'll call you in the morning."

As Tony was driving his sister to the family home in Dartmouth, Melissa suggested that she should postpone her wedding plans.

Tony disagreed, "We'll all pitch in to help you. Don't take this all on yourself or feel guilty that happened to her. Plus, your wedding is still three months away."

Maria O'Malley did her best to reassure her daughters, Margaret and Julia that their grandmother would soon recover from her injuries. "We are so fortunate that your aunt Deo is a nurse," she said. "She could understand what the doctor was saying and she will help us to give Vavó the treatment she will need once she leaves the hospital."

"When can we see Vavó?" asked Margaret. "Right now, your vavó needs to rest," answered her mother.

Daniel O'Malley suggested, "By the weekend I think they will be encouraging us to visit your grandmother. Your happy faces will be a strong medicine for her."

Julia added, "Margaret and I said a rosary while waiting for you to come home. We even lit a candle before the statue of Our Lady of Fatima. Margaret was very careful in lighting the candle and we blew it out as soon as we finished."

After a quick supper of kale soup, that Maria had prepared earlier in the day, and some Pop rolls, Julia related that she had been chosen for the role of Laurey in the school musical, *Oklahoma*.

Excitedly Julia added, "Chris Dupont was chosen to play the part of Curly. He is such a dreamboat with his black curly hair. We sing a couple of songs together. We just started practicing: 'People will say we're in love.' There's plenty of dancing too."

After so much anxiety over Vavó, Julia's enthusiasm made everyone smile. Maria could just picture Julia with her long, wavy red hair singing opposite the spirited young man who frequently walked by their house on his way to the corner market. They would make quite a pair on stage.

Later that night Tony called the O'Malley household and spoke with his sister Maria, "Deo just called me. Her shift supervisor gave her the OK to make a quick visit to see Vavó. She is resting comfortably. She wanted to reassure us before we went to bed."

Two by Each
Book Nine

Two by Each
Book Nine

Chapter Thirty-nine

Coming together

During the summer months Claude and Anne Lepage were experiencing some respite after their first hectic Lenten season at the fish and chip restaurant. Their work at the restaurant was now reduced to three days. Thursday was prep day with sales sharply reduced. Friday was steady and profitable. Saturday's sales ended earlier so that they cleaned up before leaving in the evening and had Sunday off.

Anne now had some quiet time to read her novels. Years earlier she had found a quiet shady spot at the rear of the six family tenement building. The rear entrance on the north side of the building that the Saulnier family shared with the other tenants was rarely used. Everyone used the front entrance. Each morning she would put fresh water into the bird bath and added bird seeds when necessary.

In the morning hours the three story building provided shade, and as the sun rose she would move her chair under a medium sized crabapple tree that seemed to thrive in the small back yard. During spring and early summer before the heat became uncomfortable pink aromatic blossoms filled the tree. Anne just loved it. While she read quietly, the birds would frequent the feeder and drink and wash themselves in the bird bath.

Anne's principal had agreed that she could develop a new syllabus for her class at Normandin Junior High. She had chosen the works of Alexandre Dumas. Everyone was still talking about the

Technicolor adventure film adapted from his classic novel, the *Three Musketeers* that had come out a few years earlier. Her hope was that her students would go beyond the exciting fighting choreography in the combat scenes and the love triangle between Gene Kelly, June Allyson and the devious Lana Turner and learn to appreciate the rhetoric and language skill of the author.

Anne thoroughly enjoyed the company of her sister-in-law, Martha. Anne told her, "I've encouraged my next year students to begin reading *The Count of Monte Cristo* during the summer. Along with a great historical setting it also contains themes of hope, justice, vengeance and forgiveness. Dumas' writings are so colorful and flow so smoothly."

Listening to Anne's impassioned and moving description of the author, Martha had exclaimed, "You've convinced me. I'm going to buy one of Dumas' novels. Then I'll go to the library and read the rest of his works. I'll share my reactions with you."

Anne encouraged Martha, "You might want to keep a little journal of your impressions and reactions. That's what I require my students to do. Not only are they reinforcing their recollection for the future, but they are unknowingly improving their writing skills. So often I see my students capturing the skill and techniques of the different authors in their reflections."

The discussion about the Count of Monte Cristo had triggered something in Martha. She shared with Anne, "I'm concerned about Mortimer Weigand. The feeling that he is alive has been reinforced by your synopsis of the Count's story. My original thought was that he had lost his grip on reality. However, what Claude told me about his years of working with him contrast sharply with that thought. He's an extremely clever and resourceful person. There is something mysterious going on here."

Two by Each
Chapter Forty

Within a few months after their return from San Francisco, Barbara O'Toole had obtained a nursing position at the growing Myles Standish School for the Mentally Retarded located in her hometown of Taunton. Martha Lepage was still awaiting word about her application at St. Luke's Hospital. At her interview she had learned that the only opening available was in the pediatric ward. The interview team had agreed with her request for a position in the surgical and emergency area of the hospital. It would be more in keeping with her experience in the Navy hospitals. Each week the two friends would try to get together depending on Barbara's still irregular schedule. After all, she was the new nurse in the wards.

The O'Toole family owned a small cottage on West Island. It was located at the tip of Sconticut Neck in Fairhaven. This turned out to be a great place to spend time together. One summer evening as they watched the sun set over the cove, Barbara mentioned, "I didn't realize that this large area of Taunton was converted into a military staging area during the War. It was developed as the Boston Port of Embarkation where American soldiers as well as soldiers from Canada and Australia were processed before engaging in the European Theater. Unknown to the local citizens, a large number of German soldiers who were captured during the war were also detained at the camp."

Barbara continued, "The camp closed almost immediately after the end of the war. For a brief period Camp Myles Standish was considered as a possible site for the United Nations. When that didn't materialize, Massachusetts took over the site. Persons with mental disabilities were originally housed in the hospital area of the former army camp. A few years ago Governor Dever was instrumental in building a dozen brick buildings on the south part of the campus. That's the area where I work. However, we still have a former surgery theater in one of the older wooden barracks. I occasionally assist in some of the minor operations still conducted there on the patients."

Martha commented, "Your recounting of the history of the School for the Mentally Retarded brings back memories of my work at the Oakland Naval Hospital. In that case, the War Department took over a golf course in the Oak Knoll section of Oakland that commanded a great view of the Bay. Barracks had been constructed quickly so that we could provide medical care to the increasing number of wounded Marine and Navy personnel returning from the Pacific front."

Over the previous few weeks, Barbara had been introducing Martha to different activities available on West Island. She said, "Tomorrow looks like a great day for quahogging. We have a low tide around nine in the morning. We'll have sufficient time to dig for the clams and get cleaned up in time for me to drop you off at your house and head up back to Taunton to make my night shift. I have to report by six o'clock."

Martha was a city girl and wasn't accustomed to the muddy marshes that circled the island. She tried to go along with Barbara's evident excitement. She said to Barbara, "The rubber covering for my feet that you bought me should help to keep the muck from getting between my toes. I'm still not comfortable with the feel of seaweed wrapping around my legs as we venture out into the cove, but I'm willing to give it another try. Then maybe I might try another raw little neck on the shell. I especially liked the way you steamed them with onions, corn on the cob and linguica. That's a tasty treat."

Aware that Martha was squeamish in the marshes; Barbara selected an area for clamming that led to a sandy section. Barbara reminded her to watch as she walked over this area. "I'm heading for that section over there. See the lighter, grey area to my right. That's a

174

sandy strip caused by the shifting tides. It's easier to scratch for quahogs in that area of the bay and the clams are cleaner with less mud around them."

The walk into the water was a bit treacherous but once they reached the sandy strip which was less than waist high, Martha exclaimed, "I like this. I can see the bottom and there's no seaweed around with hidden crabs to frighten me."

"Here, take the rake," stated Barbara. "Hold it lightly and pull back toward yourself. You don't have to dig deeply into the sand. The clams are just below the surface. When you feel that you've hit some obstacle, let me know."

In less than a minute, Martha said, "I feel something!"

Barbara, who had wandered off a bit, came over. "Now move your rake back a little bit and put a little more pressure into the sand. Do you still feel it?"

"Yes," answered Martha.

"Now, reach the rake under it and lift it up slowly to the surface," instructed Barbara. As the sand washed away, a good sized quahog remained on the teeth of the rake. "I did it!" exclaimed Martha and in her excitement the clam fell back into the water. "Oh, no!"

"Stay calm and don't move too much," said Barbara. "We don't want to stir the waters. The clam will still be on the surface. However, they don't fall straight down. The water we are standing in is quite clear and we may be able to spot it and pick it back up and put it in the basket."

Both looked for a short spell. Barbara eventually put her face into the water in order to see more clearly. When she came back up, she said, "I see it. There's clam a foot or so next to your right foot. Search for it with the rake."

"I feel something," said Martha.

"Go under it again and bring it up slowly." There was Martha's prize possession. "Take hold of it and place it into the basket," said Barbara. She had a wire basket with a Styrofoam ring attached to it keeping the basket afloat. "You are now an official quahogger," affirmed Martha. "Keep doing what I showed you and I'll go to a place nearby that is shallower and dig with my fingers."

Before Barbara had found a spot, Martha was shouting with excitement, "I found another one." Both kept busy and before long the basket was close to half full. Barbara showed Martha the metal ring that was attached to the basket. "We can only keep quahogs that are large enough to keep from passing through the ring at the wide side of the shell," instructed Martha. She showed Barbara the shape of the clam and how to size it properly. Most of the time we can visually determine the keepers. The smaller ones we leave behind so that they can grow to the proper size."

Once back to the shore, Barbara poked around into the basket and felt quite confident that their catch contained the proper size clams. They walked back to the cottage, greeting a few neighbors who had remained on the island. Most island dwellers came on the weekends and returned to their homes and work by Sunday evening. Occasionally families would stay for a week's vacation, especially around the fourth of July and Labor Day when many mills still closed shop for those holidays.

There was a long handled pump attached to the well at the back of the building. There the women washed the clams clean and placed them in a container. They rinsed off their rubberized shoes, the wire basket and rake and put them out to dry. Martha had previously instructed Martha that rinsing off the salt water was important to keeping the metal parts from rusting.

The previous day they had filled a large black rubber ball shaped container with water. A spout at one end had been closed and securely fastened. Then the black ball had been lifted by rope to a secure spot in an enclosure that provided privacy for an outdoor shower. Sunlight hitting the exposed black water container would provide a warm shower after a day at the beach.

While still in her bathing attire, Barbara went into the cottage and brought the linguica and corn that she brought to the island and stored in the ice box of the small kitchen. On their trip to the island they had purchased a small block of ice from a variety store on the Neck. Barbara had shaved off some of the ice with an ice pick and placed the food items in the chest lined with metal that served as their refrigerator. Most of the block was kept intact so as to provide a cold compartment for as long as possible.

Martha followed instructions carefully. They placed some water in the bottom of the pan that would provide steam for cooking. The clams were placed first and then the onions with chunks of linguica and ears of fresh corn. In the meantime, Barbara started a fire in a small outdoor pit that had a metal grate extended over the rocks. There they placed the pan for boiling.

"Let me take a quick shower," commented Barbara. "Then I'll watch our dinner, while you shower. It doesn't take long for this meal to cook, once the steam starts. We don't want to overcook the quahogs. They can get tough."

Both dressed in loose housecoats, the women almost drooled as they enjoyed the results of their labors. Reluctantly, they were too soon driving over the causeway back to civilization. Barbara was in her nurse uniform and at the wheel of her Chevrolet.

Two by Each
Chapter Forty-one

Inspector O'Malley met with Detective Joe Barrett on a very hot and humid morning in late July. The windows in the inspector's office were wide open and an electric fan was circulating the already muggy air around the room. "This is going to be another hot one," commented O'Malley. "It's not eight o'clock yet, and everything is dripping.

Joe Barrett nodded in agreement. His breathing was labored. "This air is not good for my asthma. The newspaper this morning was advising people with respiratory problems to limit any strenuous activity. They blamed the poor air quality on high amounts of ground-level ozone."

The inspector stated, "I received a call from Bill Normandin. The FBI agency had set up a drop off point with Mortimer. Every other Friday a certain amount of cash was placed secretly at that spot. These funds helped support his operation. Cash dropped off on the Friday before Mortimer's hanging was uncovered by Claude Lepage. On the next delivery date two weeks later, they found that these funds had not been retrieved. Normandin instructed his people to remove those funds when they went back there yesterday. If Mortimer is alive, he decided not pick up this money. Normandin ventured that this would make sense in the light that Mortimer seemed to suspect that the mole in his operation was internal to the FBI."

Joe Barrett reflected, "This information does not provide direct proof that Mortimer is alive or dead. I like hard evidence. We continue to conjecture a lot in this case."

"What did you find out?" asked O'Malley. Joe Barrett answered, "I went through the material we found in Mortimer's office at his home and on the waterfront. In his home office, I found a little used checkbook and a savings account pass book. On the first of each month an amount of $400.00 was deposited into his saving account. I don't know the source of these funds. The checks issued were primarily for household expenses. There was no evidence that Mortimer paid for the salaries of his employees."

O'Malley added, "Mr. Willard may be able to enlighten us on this matter. I have requested information from him about Mortimer's finances with the bank and the trusts that he administers for the Spooner family. He is scheduled to meet with me tomorrow afternoon."

"Did you find any cash among Mortimer's belongings?" inquired O'Malley. "Just the few coins that were discovered in his desk drawer," answered Barrett.

"Mortimer must have had a place to keep the cash that he received from the FBI," speculated Barrett. He continued, "I dislike this type of approach to a case, but that's seems to be the only avenue open to us."

"I agree," said O'Malley. "Between the time he retrieved the money and used it in his operation, he had to have stashed it away in some safe place. We know he assisted fishermen to upgrade their radio navigation systems. We also know that Carlos Frias in the South End informed us that he did some of that work. Find out what boats he worked on that had been directed to Carlos' business by Mortimer. See if you can find out from the owners or operators of these vessels how these transactions occurred. It had to be in cash. See if you can uncover a trend, a particular meeting place, anything that may point to the safe place he kept his stash of funds. There's a good chance that there is still some cash hidden in that place."

O'Malley cautioned Barrett, "Don't overdo it. Working around the docks can be strenuous. Keep yourself hydrated."

Two by Each
Chapter Forty-two

Inspector O'Malley's meetings with Mr. Willard, the bank president, had begun to be more pleasant and O'Malley hoped that Mr. Willard would continue to be forthcoming about information relating to Mortimer. Mr. Willard's secretary warmly welcomed the inspector and informed him, "I received a call from Mr. Willard about ten minutes ago telling me to inform you that he was being delayed. He asked me to apologize for any inconvenience this may cause you. He asked that I inquire as to whether you may be able to meet with him later this afternoon. We quickly reviewed his schedule over the telephone and he is offering to make himself available at four. Is that a possibility for you, Inspector?"

After a few minutes consideration, O'Malley answered, "I will make a few adjustments to my afternoon schedule and will return to the bank by four." O'Malley walked back to his office. A front had moved into the local area in the overnight hours, bringing some heavy downpours and lowering the humidity quite considerably. The sun which would break through the many puffy clouds was hot but bearable.

Detective Joe Barrett was surprised to see the inspector climbing up the stairs to his office. They had prearranged to meet the following morning. Joe came out of the office he shared with other detectives and asked O'Malley, "Can you afford me some time this afternoon? I've made some interesting discoveries."

O'Malley invited him into his office. After relating the change in his schedule, the inspector inquired, "What did you discover?" "Carlos Frias turned out to be quite a source of information," began Joe. He quickly listed boat owners who had been sent to him by Mortimer. One of the owners was Arthur Lerner who owns two fishing boats and one of them is named The Puffin. That name struck a bell. It was part of your report when you visited his home and learned that Mr. Lerner had provided a ride to Mortimer from the Wamsutta Club to his office on the waterfront the night before the discovery of Mortimer and his subsequent disappearance."

"That is interesting," agreed the inspector.

"When I saw that The Puffin was tied up at the pier, I even became a little excited," continued Joe. "The cleaner air today has helped with my breathing and even an old buck like me can experience the thrill of the hunt. Two men were on the vessel cleaning and tidying things up. Mr. Lerner was one of those men."

"He's a rough and bristly guy," commented Joe. "When I called out from the pier next to the boat, he started to climb out of it and when I offered a hand so that he could climb out more easily, he pushed my hand aside. I told him that I was trying to learn of his business dealings with Mr. Mortimer Weigand. His eyes didn't waver but he did turn and told the other person on board to keep up the work and that he would be back shortly."

"He brought me to a small shed at the top of the pier," continued Joe Barrett. "He called it his office. There was a table that could serve as a desk and only one chair with the back broken off. The room had a small window that was shut and covered with metal bars. Only the open door provided light and some ventilation. There was a heavy smell of fish, sweat and oil filling the room. I could feel my lungs struggling for air. So I asked if we could step outside. He gave me a look of disgust and he led me to a quiet spot."

"What did you learn?" asked an impatient O'Malley.

"He was surprised that I knew that he was part of a special observation group," added Barrett. "He also admitted that Mortimer Weigand had provided funds for the radio controls on his fishing boats. He agreed that they were cash transactions. The money was never transacted hand to hand. The cash was always wrapped in a newspaper and he would retrieve it from an agreed upon location, a different one each time."

"Were you able to establish any rhythm in the choice of these drop off spots?" asked O'Malley.

"No," replied Barrett. "But one thought kept nagging at me. That is, I doubted if Mortimer himself would personally conduct those cash deals. One of his office men or even his chauffeur might have been involved and without even knowing what was being transacted. And the more I thought of that element, the more I began to suspect that Claude Lepage would have been the perfect unsuspecting pawn. So I went to see him. He admitted that he had made some pickups and deliveries for Mr. Weigand, his boss. The pickups were made at a post office box in the downtown post office. Any deliveries that were wrapped in a newspaper were made to different locations, usually in the hallway adjacent to office buildings where his boss had frequent meetings, including the rear entrance of the Wamsutta Club."

Joe Barrett continued, "Claude estimated that he began picking up brown manila envelopes from the post office over a year ago. He would go there every other Tuesday on the way back to Mr. Weigand's home on Mechanics Lane. They would arrive there before five. Mortimer would give him the key to the box. Claude indicated that he never saw the contents of the envelope."

The inspector asked, "Did we ever find any keys among Mortimer's possessions? And if so, did we try to identify the lock to which each key would belong to?"

"We did find a small key ring in Mortimer's top drawer of his desk at this home," answered Barrett. "The keys Mortimer would have used to enter his office on the docks were found in the suit jacket left behind in his office. I'll check to see if the keys on the ring were checked out. There may be one that matches the type of key used at the post office."

O'Malley questioned the detective, "Did Claude suspect the contents of the deliveries he made for Mortimer?"

"No," answered Barrett quickly. "Claude thought that he was delivering some newspaper item about the fishing business. He suspected that Mortimer was bringing this information to the attention of one of his business associates. These deliveries were always made at noon and always at a different location. Claude commented that the newspaper was always folded the same way. He guessed that it contained only about five pages, even when the daily paper is normally much larger. The newspaper was placed on the floor inside the entrances. On a few occasions he was delayed by meeting someone he knew outside the building. He then would see different persons enter the building and quickly exit with the newspaper tucked under the armpit."

"Did he recognize any of these people?" asked O'Malley.

"I asked that question," answered Barrett. "He said all of them were dressed as dock workers or fishermen, and not the business men that Mortimer usually met at his meetings. On one occasion he remembered thinking that he recognized one of them but that was a long time ago and he couldn't bring that recollection back to mind."

"All these discoveries that you have made are in keeping with Agent Bill Normandin's description of Mortimer's clandestine operation," commented the inspector. "One thing that strikes me is that there was a lot of cash involved. That would support the theory that someone had gotten wind of this and was trying to discover where the loot was hidden when Mortimer arrived unexpectedly at his office at the dock that ill-fated Sunday evening."

Detective Joe Barrett agreed and added, "The only fact that contradicts these assumptions is that Claude's sister received a letter from Mortimer at her previous address on the West Coast that is postmarked a week after this incident. Also, why would someone remove the body from the scene once it had been seen? These two facts continue to baffle me."

Two by Each
Chapter Forty-three

Inspector O'Malley returned to the Whaling City National Bank and greeted the elevator attendant who brought him to the top floor of the bank. The receptionist upon recognizing him entering her office immediately rose from her chair and escorted him to the bank president's office.

Mr. Anthony Willard was profusely apologetic, "Please accept my regret for not keeping my appointment with you earlier today. An unexpected and critical business matter had been brought to my attention. I was informed that a principle in this venture had sustained serious injuries in a motor vehicle accident last night. I personally visited the hospital in Providence where he was being treated. We were at a critical stage in the financing of a major infrastructure project for our city. I needed to reassure myself that the accident was as serious as it was reported, and not just a delaying tactic. The person had in fact sustained head injuries but was conscious. Though groggy from drugs, that person was able to convince me that the project would continue as scheduled."

"Enough about my concerns," continued Mr. Willard. "You indicated to me in your communication over the telephone that you were inquiring about Mortimer Weigand's financial affairs. How may I assist you?"

The inspector related, "We have discovered two bank accounts in Mortimer's name. The saving account received a monthly deposit of $400.00 on the first of each month. We were ..." Mr. Willard interrupted, "That amount is deposited into Mortimer's account from his trust fund for ordinary expenses. The trust fund also pays all his regular expenses of the household, including salaries, utilities, etc. Mortimer is quite frugal. I would suspect that those monthly funds are accumulating in his account."

For the first time, O'Malley shared something of the operation that Mortimer was conducting under the auspices of the FBI. O'Malley sensed that the bank president was quite disturbed with this revelation. Mr. Willard stated, "I'm disappointed that Mortimer did not share this information with me, and more so that he used our business transactions as a cover for this other operation."

When O'Malley explained that the FBI undertaking was funded with cash, Mr. Willard was almost fuming. "Mortimer dared to question my business dealings which would take advantage of a person's weakness, but he did the same with me. He took advantage of my attachment to him."

O'Malley tried to bring the interview back to his concerns. He told the bank president of the chauffeur's admitted role in the transactions. O'Malley asked, "Do you have any suspicions about the three men who worked with Mortimer? Would any of them have turned on Mortimer if they discovered that a considerable amount of cash had been available to him?"

Mr. Willard answered briefly, "Mortimer had chosen his own team. Of course, I also conducted my own inquiries as to the character and reliability of these men. I had been satisfied with his choices. However, money has the power to infect even the most righteous."

O'Malley continued, "We have confirmed where the FBI dropped off the funds for this covert operation, as well as how it was distributed. A question remains: where were these funds held between transactions?"

"I cannot offer a solution to that question," answered an agitated Mr. Willard, "especially as Mortimer kept me in the dark about this."

The next morning Joe Barrett met again with the inspector. He offered some additional findings. "One of Mortimer's keys did match those used at the central post office. The number inscribed on the key allowed us to open the box and, as I suspected from Bill Normandin's earlier statement to us, it was empty. I was able to locate the cancelled checks that Mortimer wrote from his account. Each week a check was written to cash and with the notation - groceries. I went back over a two year period. A few other checks were written to various clothing stores in the city. A little over a year ago, Mortimer wrote some checks to New Bedford Shoe Repair. All seems in keeping with his lifestyle and the special shoes that he was required to wear. When the checking account funds began to run low, he would simply transfer funds from his savings account."

O'Malley told Barrett, "I will contact Bill Normandin and find out from him how the need for cash was related back to him and the amounts. In the meantime, follow up on the places where Mortimer wrote his checks. It surprised me that Mortimer kept Mr. Willard in the dark, especially in the context of the bank president's candid affection for him. We need to learn as much as we can about Mortimer."

Two by Each
Chapter Forty-four

Early one morning Al Lepage quietly closed the door of his tenement behind him. He had kissed his wife Janet goodbye. She had a rare Monday morning off from her waitress job at her brother's restaurant on the avenue. His three children were sleeping soundly and they would awaken to the joy of having their mother with them for the entire day. She said to Al "I'm planning to take the children to the park later today. The fire department has been placing water sprinklers in the ice skating rink so that the children of the neighborhood can cool off. These tenements are placed so close to one another that they hardly catch a cooling breeze. There is so little ventilation."

As Al quickly went down the three flights of stairs, he reflected on his wonderful Janet who met any possible misfortune with a creative and calming solution. He was truly blessed.

The hot and humid days of August had descended on the city. Already the early sunrises that had greeted Al just a few weeks earlier were getting later each day. At five o'clock dawn was now only slowly creeping into the sky. There was a heavy mist in the air, and the sun wouldn't rise over the horizon for another hour. Al reflected, "It will take some time before the sun burns off the fog rising from the river." Early morning chirping from the birds in the neighborhood greeted Al. He loved this time of day.

All day long Al spent his day talking with people. He loved to hear their stories and happenings. People just as easily shared their burdens as their triumphs with him. He was non-judgmental and accepted the fact that everyone had strengths and weaknesses.

Men as well as women revealed very personal issues with him. He was a good listener.

Now the early morning hours on his way to pick up his orders at the various bakeries, was his quiet time. He loved to reminisce. The evening before his sister Martha had joined his family for a special treat at Frates Dairy. They served the best homemade ice cream in the city. Sitting in the shade of the large milk bottle building added a distinctive flavor to the licking of their ice cream cones.

Al was glad to see how Martha and his eldest daughter, Charlotte, got along. While eating their ice cream, they had moved away from the others. Charlotte had always been the responsible one. She kept a vigilant eye on her younger brother and sister. She had exclaimed to her mother as she prepared for bed, "Martha is just great. We talked about so many things, especially what I would like to do now that I'm entering high school. She treats me like an adult, listens to my dreams and encourages me to reach for the sky. Those are the words she used."

Martha had also told him that while waiting for an opening in the emergency or surgery department at St. Luke's Hospital that she had made an application to return to the Navy as a member of the Naval Reserves. She had already been assured that her application would be accepted. "I'm just waiting for the final details of my monthly assignments to be worked out. I will be a nurse instructor to the Corpsmen who serve in the Reserves. I just loved working with the Navy Corpsmen during my assignments at the Newport and Oakland Naval Hospitals."

Over the weekend there had been a totally unexpected conversation with one of his brothers. Jean Paul had revealed to him, "Only Ma knows so far, but I've been talking with a priest at the LaSalette Shrine in Attleboro. I love my carpentry work with Mr.

Medeiros, my new car and my friends and all you guys, but I feel something inside me is searching for more. I've always found a certain peace in the quiet of a church or an occasional walk in the woods. Fr. Paquin says that it seems to him that these yearnings are similar to religious meditation and prayer. He's encouraging me to spend a year at their place in New Hampshire, a property the LaSalette missionary group bought about twenty-five years ago. It previously belonged to the Shakers who lived a simple and communal life. It overlooks Mascoma Lake in Enfield. He called it a peaceful place. I would contribute my woodworking skills as they are in the process of building a shrine to Our Lady similar to the one in Attleboro, and join the other community members in a life of prayer. In the future I could be assigned to one of their foreign missions. That part also attracts me."

Jean Paul continued, "I'm concerned about the car the family bought. I'm paying half of the monthly loan payments and we still have more than a year to go. Plus, I keep the gas tank full."

Al encouraged his brother, "The family will manage somehow. We usually do. Don't forget your sister Martha is home now. She'll be getting a good paying job soon and from what she told me she has some savings. Plus she likes having the family car available for her use, too."

Two by Each
Chapter Forty-five

Detective Joe Barrett had spent a quiet weekend. His wife, Catherine, had died of breast cancer a few years before. Their only daughter had married and had moved to upstate New York with her husband and two boys. Joe Barrett had sold the family home. It was a simple cottage nestled among the many tenement houses on Earle Street, above Ashley Boulevard. He now lived in a rooming house not far from the main police station. He could walk to work and pick up an unmarked police car when he needed one.

Joe was saving his money. He was planning to retire within the year and his daughter had invited him to move in with them where the country air of upstate New York would help his asthma. Her two young sons, Bobby and Peter, were all enthused about this plan and awaited the day when he would again be part of their family. Joe Barrett was determined that he would help solve the case of the missing Mortimer Weigand before going out on retirement.

On Monday morning Joe Barrett informed O'Malley that he had made an unexpected discovery. "The clothing retailers that Mortimer had frequented did not provide any assistance in solving the case. However, much to my surprise, the cobbler who fixed Mortimer's special shoes stated that Mortimer had requested a major change in the design. Both shoes retained the same fitting to support his ankles but a compartment had been added to the sides. They were made of the same black material and were hardly noticeable to anyone looking at them. From the cobbler's description of the size of these compartments, Mortimer could easily have hidden some cash in them. He kept his cash close to him."

O'Malley added, "That may explain why Mortimer was removed from his office. Someone may have discovered, just before Claude Lepage came on the scene, that the cash was hidden in Mortimer's special shoes. Why not just remove the money and run? That's also a good question."

Joe Barrett suggested an answer, "Mr. Perrone, the cobbler, was proud to show me the very meticulous details of the new design of Mortimer's shoes. The hidden compartments were sealed by a very recent invention of a hook and loop fastener developed by a Swiss engineer. He named it Velcro, a combination of the French words *velours* (velvet) and *crochet* (hook). Lastly, the shoes had to be removed before the fastener could be pulled apart and opened. Claude's description of the scene includes the detail that Mortimer was hanging from the ceiling with his shoes on."

O'Malley conjectured, "This helps to support one theory that Mortimer's secret cache of funds made him a target of foul play. It could also be a reason why the body was removed from the scene. The criminal still hadn't found a way to remove the cash."

In the meantime, in his office at the top floor of the bank, Mr. Anthony Willard was conducting his own investigation. Over the weekend, his anger and disappointment with Mortimer Weigand had slowly dissipated. He began to appreciate the value of the clandestine operation that Mortimer was conducting for his country. Reluctantly, he even allowed himself to admit that Mortimer's operation which was not shared with him spoke to the significance of his project, and not a personal affront to their filial relationship. With renewed fervor and energy, he committed himself to unearthing the mystery behind Mortimer's disappearance.

Mr. Willard had eventually closed down Mortimer's operation at the docks. Without Mortimer's synopsis and analysis of the material collected by his three man staff, the information was no longer helpful in the making of financial decisions. He had given the men a good severance pay to assist them until they were able to discover other employment.

Inspector Daniel O'Malley's question about the reliability of Mortimer's team needed to be confirmed. Russ Oliver, the private detective hired by the bank and Mr. Willard, was presenting the results of his investigation. Russ always reported his findings in person and without any written material. He concluded his presentation, "There is no reason to suggest that these men had turned on their boss. During their work for him and even now after their termination, their lives do not support any major change of lifestyle. Only one required some additional scrutiny. He was known as quite a drinker at the bars around the docks. However, it gives credence to what Mortimer had indicated to you in his reports, that he used that ploy to loosen the tongues of workers in the fishing industry. He was the first of the men to get a job. He now works at an auto dealership polishing cars and no longer frequents any drinking establishments."

The bank president thanked Russ for his work and passed an envelope across the desk. Russ folded the envelope in two and slipped it inside his back pocket, saying, "Thank you, Mr. Willard. I'm always ready to be of service to you."

"There is another person that I want you to investigate," stated Mr. Willard. After a brief account of the person, Russ put on his grey cap and exited the office.

Mr. Willard still had to reassure himself about one other individual and that was Claude Lepage. Claude had been one of the most trusted members of Mortimer's staff. In addition this whole affair hinged upon Claude's testimony. Within weeks of his dismissal, Mr. Willard learned that Claude had purchased and opened a restaurant in the North End of the city. How did he finance such a venture?

Mr. Willard's secretary, Carol Walker, had researched the purchase and sale agreement and had provided him with her report. He was perusing this material and learned that the recently formed Merchant Bank on Coffin Avenue had provided the loan. He reached for the buzzer under his desk. Carol Walker opened the glass door to the office and walked in.

"You require my services?" inquired Mrs. Walker.

"Yes," answered the bank president, "get me the name of the president of the Merchant Bank and his personal line at this office or even at his home if necessary."

Mrs. Walker nodded and retreated to her office.

Less than ten minutes later, Carol Walker knocked on Mr. Willard's office door. He asked her to enter and she related what she had found, "The bank on Coffin Avenue is one of the branch offices of the Merchant Bank with its home office in Brockton. The bank president is Thomas Quinlan who lives in Stoughton, MA, but who is presently away on a business trip to the Carolinas. I did get the name and telephone number of the branch manager. His name is Mr. Ronald Poirier. He is a young local man with a growing family. This is his first job as a branch manager. He originally worked at the Institution for Savings and was induced to take this job by Mr. Quinlan himself at a commanding salary."

Not accustomed to speaking with branch managers from other banks, he assigned it to Mrs. Walker, "Call Mr. Poirier on my behalf inquiring as to the nature of the loan that Claude Lepage has received from the bank especially as to any down payment and collateral. Let him know it is a personal favor and will be repaid."

Miss Esmeralda Aguiar, known as Essi by her associates at work, answered the telephone at the Coffin Avenue branch of the Merchant Bank. Essi informed Mr. Willard's secretary, "Mr. Poirier is occupied at the moment with a client. If you provide me with your name and telephone number, he will return your call as soon as he is free."

Essi was one of the four bank tellers at the branch. The neighborhood that had been mostly of French Canadian ancestry was beginning to change. Families of Portuguese ancestry, especially from the Azorean Islands were moving into the homes of the area. Many of the elder members of these families spoke little or no English. Essi had just completed her senior year at New Bedford High on County Street. She had been hired by the Bank and assigned to Mr. Poirier because of her fluency in speaking Portuguese. At home only Portuguese was spoken.

Essi had lived a sheltered and protected life within her family. Even during her high school years, all her classmates were well scrutinized. At her interview with Mr. Poirier, her father and older brother who served as translator had interrogated him respectfully but with determination. Mr. Aguiar was not about to send his first born daughter out into this business world without an assurance that she would be safe.

Ronald Poirier smiled and tried to assuage Mr. Aguiar's anxiety, "I have a daughter who graduated from New Bedford High last year and she is now a freshman at Stonehill College in Easton. I did some exhaustive study of the school, the campus, and the living arrangements for the women students." Ronald spoke slowly as Essi's older brother needed to translate this message for his father. He thought it was important to share with the Aguiars that the Holy Cross Religious Order, who had established the already prestigious University of Notre Dame in the mid-west, had opened this Catholic college just outside of Brockton less than ten years prior. Mr. Poirier added, "The small college admitted its first women students only a few years ago. Right now they represent only about twenty percent of the student population. Last year they had their first coed graduating class."

Mr. Poirier looked directly into Mr. Aguiar's eyes, "My oldest daughter, Constance, is also very precious to me. She had excellent marks in high school. She thinks she may want to become a doctor. We are making great sacrifices in order to provide her with this opportunity. Very importantly, we want her to be safe. She's a good girl and we need to trust her."

Mr. Aguiar interrupted his son as he tried to translate for him. He had seen into the eyes of a good man, a father who cared for his family. Haltingly he spoke, "I trust you with my Esmeralda."

When Essi saw the bank client exiting Mr. Poirier's office, she excused herself from the line of tellers and informed Mr. Poirier of the call that she had received while he was occupied. She presented him with a note that contained all the pertinent information.

Ronald was a bit curious as to why the personal secretary of the bank president of the Whaling City National Bank would be calling him. On the second ring, Mrs. Walker identified herself. Ronald began, "This is Mr. Poirier of the Merchant Bank."

Carol immediately replied, "Thank you for returning my call so promptly. Mr. Willard, the bank president, has discovered that your president, Thomas Quinlan, is presently out of the area on business. Mr. Willard is seeking information about the details of a small loan that was executed by your branch. He has some dealings with this Mr. Claude Lepage and would be very appreciative for any enlightenment of your proceedings so as to guide him."

Ronald's curiosity was piqued as it was a rather out of the ordinary request. But he thought, "Bank presidents probably share such information with some frequency as a courtesy to each other." He answered, "I do remember the occasion of this loan. Let me retrieve the file and see if I can be of assistance to your president, Mr. Willard." Ronald had written down a few notes during the telephone conversation.

Mr. Poirier had only originated a few loans in his post as director of the branch. He was still learning the process and was being guided by personnel at the main office. He opened the thin folder and inquired, "Mrs. Walker, I have the loan document for a Mr. Claude Lepage. As you know too well, some of this information is considered confidential. How may I assist you?"

Mrs. Carol Walker explained, "From public records we know that a loan was made to Mr. Lepage by your bank as well as its amount in order to purchase a restaurant in the north end of the city. Our president, Mr. Willard, is seeking to know how this loan was secured so that his own dealings with Mr. Lepage are not compromised."

"I see," answered a rather uneasy Ronald Poirier. "Let me look into the file," he added. In his mind he was attempting to assure himself that a bank president would not be seeking this information without good reason. "The records show that Mr. Lepage secured his loan with a down payment of $350.00, in cash."

Mrs. Walker continued, "Was there any other collateral?" "No," answered Ronald. "References and the amount of the down payment were deemed sufficient by our people who reviewed the loan."

Two by Each
Book Ten

Two by Each
Book Ten

Chapter Forty-six

Finishing Touches

Two days later Russ Oliver entered the Whaling City National Bank. Early in the morning was his regular meeting time with the bank president. Only a few bank employees were present. The head teller and chief loan officer could be observed through the glass doors just returning from their first duty of the day – opening the bank vault.

Russ took the elevator to the top floor and indicated to the attendant, "My meeting should be brief. Unless you have other duties or calls for service, you may want to wait for me."

The attendant responded, "An attorney who has an office on the third floor routinely arrives at this hour. Just press the bell button on the side of the door and I'll be up to get you in a flash."

A young man dressed in a black suit with a white shirt and black bow tie had recently replaced the well-revered Mr. Franklin. He had been the elevator attendant of the bank building ever since the elevator had been installed. His health had recently declined and he had begun to allow himself to sit on a small stool while awaiting passengers for his elevator. For years he had always stood at attention near the elevator for hours on end.

The new elevator attendant with the name Jimmy sewn on his suit jacket pocket seemed very uncomfortable in this type of dress. He kept pulling at his bow tie which often slipped down on one side. Mrs. Carol Walker had commented on it just that morning.

This gave him an opportunity to suggest a solution that had come to his mind in the first few days of work at the bank, "Do you think it would be permissible to wear a regular tie rather than this unwieldy bow tie? It would be much more fashionable."

She answered quickly and with some annoyance, "I will have to consult the bank president, Mr. Anthony Willard. Traditions are very important in this business. It exemplifies consistency and dependability. However, many of our newer clientele who deal directly with our president do exhibit a significant change in their attire. Dark suits have given way to lighter colors. It's appalling!"

Jimmy smiled to himself. He liked the atmosphere of his new job. He felt important just being gracious to his passengers and occasionally engaging in conversation with them. He had been well instructed by Mr. Franklin, "Always greet your passengers politely and only engage in conversation with them when they initiate it. Never gossip nor offer an opinion. Smile and listen. You'll learn a lot on this job. I may write a book someday. A few years ago I started to write some of my recollections. However, it couldn't be printed and available to the public until all the characters are deceased and even then some family members could take exception." Mr. Franklin smiled, "Whatever, it's a great way to pass my time."

Russ Oliver, the private detective, was presenting his findings to Mr. Willard. "You probably know much of this information that I have collected on Claude Lepage," he started. "I will be brief and will highlight areas that may be of interest or concern to you. Claude is a member of a large French Canadian family living in the north end of the city. The family has a good reputation with none of them having any rap sheet with the police. Claude served with the Seabees as a cook on one of the islands in the Pacific. I discovered that one of Claude's sisters was a Navy nurse on the West Coast. She had ministered to Mortimer Weigand and a friendship continued after he returned home. She was the one who had recommended Claude to be Mortimer's chauffeur. It turned out to be a good fit with both Mortimer Weigand and Claude appreciating regularity and order. Basic Navy training seemed to have instilled discipline into both of their lives."

Mr. Willard interrupted, "Mortimer had shared this element of their relationship with me. What else did you uncover that may be of interest to me?"

"I was coming to that," answered Russ Oliver. "Claude's wife is a teacher in one of the city's junior high schools. She's bashful but well respected by her peers and students. She's an only child and Claude and his wife live in the tenement of her parents. Along with Claude's work for Mr. Weigand, he had continued to work a very early morning shift as a baker in a local restaurant that served only breakfast and luncheon meals. Claude's work with Mr. Weigand always ended punctually at five. Claude returned to his neighborhood by bus and he had developed a habit of frequenting a croquet club located near the bus stop at the top of his street. During the nice weather he played croquet and I was told that he played it quite well. But the central activity of the club was that of playing cards. It was related to me that Claude was very addicted to the game of pitch. On rare occasions he extended his playing of this card game beyond six-thirty. He had members of the club trained to remind him of the time so that he would not be late for the family's evening meal. When that delay occurred, I was told that he ran down the street quite sheepishly."

Russ continued, "The club has a small, tightly knit group of members. All are from a two or three block area. As a stranger to the group, they were very circumspect with me. But as my evening with them moved on, and with the steady drinking of beer and a few shots of Four Roses whiskey, a few tongues were loosened. The bar offerings are second-rate but in keeping with the earnings of its members. I learned that Claude did not drink during the week, but on a Saturday afternoon he would keep up with the best of them. I seems that was when Claude's approach to a card game changed. He took more chances. Many referred to him as lucky. Cash gambling was not evident at the card table but outcomes of games were being tracked. I've played enough cards myself to read the hand and finger signals of a wager. One of the two bartenders did more than serve the patrons. I observed the stealthy putting down of bets with the bar man and some payments when a happy member was leaving the club."

Mr. Willard pondered these observations quietly before he spoke, "Cards and drink are a precarious combination. Plus, a sentiment of being lucky can often push one over the edge. Was there any information about Claude being in debt with any of the members? I'm attempting to track a cash trail. See if you can find any discontents among the members of the croquet club who might provide further information about Claude's financial situation."

Again Mr. Willard passed an envelope across his desk. Russ Oliver picked it up and assured the bank president that he would continue his investigation.

Two by Each
Chapter Forty-seven

The summer season was moving along rapidly. Once the Feast of the Blessed Sacrament with its colorful arches, long parade and delicious Portuguese fare was over, a whole different energy was slowly beginning to move through the city. Mothers began frequenting the smaller family owned businesses along Acushnet Avenue and the always popular downtown department stores. It was time to get the kids ready for school.

The girls who accompanied their mothers were frequently all enthused and excited in picking out a new wardrobe. The boys on the other hand just shuffled along, sometimes being pulled by the ear by a disgruntled mother. They just wanted to return to playing with friends and postpone the reality of school as long as possible.

Anne Lepage and her mother were among the shoppers. The few small tips she had received over the course of the year at the fish and chip restaurant had accumulated into a few extra dollars. She had decided that this extra money would provide a special additional touch to her teacher's apparel this school year. They were on the second floor of the Cherry and Webb store. Anne directed her mother to a rack of scarves, "Just look at these – such beautiful colors and I think the material is silk. They feel so smooth." The woman behind the counter confirmed that they were in fact made of silk. She added, "We just received this shipment a week ago. The price is higher than our other scarves but the value is in the material and the weaving of various colors of fine threads. They are going rapidly and I don't know when we will have such a quality product available again."

Anne had long flowing hair and just loved to wear a kerchief as she walked to school. She rationalized her purchase and told her mother, "This scarf I would wear to go to church, and we'll be having another baptism soon." Mrs. Saulnier accepted her daughter's decision with joy. "You work very hard, Anne. You deserve to treat yourself on occasion."

However, as the women were on the bus returning to their home, Anne began to have second thoughts about her compulsive purchase. It felt too much like self-gratification. She knew the great sacrifice her parents had made in helping Claude with the down payment for the loan that enabled them to acquire the restaurant. They had put their life's saving at their disposal. It may be too late to return the scarf but Anne resolved to focus on her parents and to continue to express her gratitude to them by the many small things she did every day.

Cora Mayfield began to advise Claude to expect a sudden surge in business once the schools reopened. She clarified, "The families will get back into their routines, and mothers will be busy with their children's homework and the additional laundry that comes with school attire. A quick and delicious evening meal will be appreciated."

One Sunday in late August Claude accompanied his brother Al on the drive to Maine to purchase a supply of potatoes. This was Claude's first trip to see and meet the suppliers. Al had recommended it after the restaurant's busy season was over but one thing or another and the summer months had flown by quickly. The trips north during that time were less frequent and Al used it as a great opportunity for the Lepage children to partake in a Sunday ride and picnic. This also freed up Janet who would visit her parents to assist her mother as her father's health deteriorated in the heat of the summer. His famous garden now consisted of only a few tomato plants and the always prolific zucchini. A few months earlier the difficult decision had been made to reduce the chicken population. For the first time in memory, new chicks were not introduced to Pepere's chicken yard.

Claude listened carefully as Al pointed out the landmarks he used to find his way to the potato fields in Maine. Al couldn't read but had a terrific memory for visual details. He stated, "Claude, it's important that someone else knows the way up north. Right now, I'm the only one who knows the way and the suppliers. Janet might be helpful as she has accompanied me on some occasions but her sense of direction is poor. If something happened to me, you could find yourself in a difficult spot."

Claude readily agreed, "I know. Sometime I take too much for granted and don't plan ahead as you do. I've always admired your sense of planning. They say the first born son takes on responsibilities more conscientiously than his younger brothers. You're my older brother and I've always depended on you being there for me. I hope I haven't taken you for granted."

This was not a usual conversation between the two brothers. Al felt a little uncomfortable and he sensed uneasiness in Claude. On occasion his leg jumped, showing that something was bothering him. Al questioned, "Is there something on your mind?"

"I'm in a bit of trouble," acknowledged Claude. "Mr. Resendes alerted us to the need to keep to a good budget plan during the summer months. We started out doing fine. We had some prior experience with budgeting since Anne's salary ends prior to summer vacation. However, I had my regular weekly income from Mr. Weigand and what I made from the Paradis luncheonette. So the adjustment was small."

"Are you behind on your payments to the bank?" inquired an anxious Al.

"No," answered Claude. "I fell behind in the payments for our weekly fish order. They have provided me one week of credit. Before I pick up this week's order, I need to pay for the supplies I picked up last week."

"Is there any way Janet and I can help you?" asked Al.

"Well, there's a little more to it than what I've told you," answered Claude. His leg was really twitching and jumping now. "Let me come clean. Since most of my day time hours at the beginning of the week are now free, I began spending more time at the croquet club. My game has really improved. I was a member of the team that won the July trophy. It wasn't the croquet that got me but playing cards. My luck ran out. When I worked for Mortimer Weigand, he paid me an extra sawbuck a week for some extra errands I did for him. That was my play money."

Al was quiet and glanced over to his brother to continue. He admitted, "Anne and I worked on the budget plans but the funds were left up to me to keep safe. So, I started taking a ten-dollar bill every once in a while, planning to replace it from my winnings. That worked for a while but as I said my luck ran out. Anne doesn't know about this situation. I've stopped going to the croquet club. I can't dig the hole any deeper. Cora has alerted me that business will be picking up rather sharply in the next couple of weeks. That means my fish orders will be larger. It will take us a while before we reap that profit and get back on an even keel."

"How much do you think you need in order to tide you over?" asked Al.

"I figure about a hundred dollars would be enough to get us over the hump," answered Claude.

"Well, I'm quite certain that's not the kind of money Janet and I have saved up for a rainy day," answered Al. "Janet is the one who puts our money away. She stretches out every dollar that I make on the bread route and adds her earnings and tips from her brother's luncheonette. I'll see what we can do to help."

Claude put out his hand and touched Al's hand on the steering wheel. "Thank you, brother. Any little bit will help, and we will pay you back. We just need a little time to get back on our feet."

"Claude can I give you a piece of advice?" When Claude gave a nod of assent, Al continued, "Don't ever keep any secret from Anne. It's better to work tough things through together than leaving your partner in the dark. You'll feel a space growing between you."

"I know what you mean, Al," agreed Claude. "I haven't had anyone to share this with for a while now. I'm beginning to feel self-conscious when I'm with Anne."

Two by Each
Chapter Forty-eight

FBI agent Bill Normandin took advantage of the Labor Day weekend visit with his family to meet with Inspector O'Malley. They met again at Thad's restaurant over lunch. They both liked the luncheon specials and the quiet dark corner tables readily available at lunch hour during the week.

O'Malley brought Bill up to speed on the investigation and was hoping to get some additional assistance from Bill. O'Malley questioned him almost as if it were the days when he was a young member of his team, "Have you been able to find a mole in Mortimer's operation?"

Bill smiled to himself. Since joining the FBI, he had discovered that most local police forces were quite circumspect and deferential in their dealings with him. They would occasionally exhibit guarded frustration, especially when as a federal agency the FBI team would insist on playing a lead role. Territorial boundaries and egos provided for a source of conflict.

Bill answered, "A careful scrutiny by internal affairs did not uncover any irregularities in the team associated with Mortimer's operation. I personally reviewed and scrutinized that report very carefully. I was the one who selected Mortimer to set up this specific arena of the national program. My research into his background, especially his years at the Naval Academy and his admirable yet abruptly terminated military career, made him a perfect candidate for this operation. I trusted his patriotism and military judgment. That's why I still struggle with his report to me of his suspicions of a leak in his operation."

O'Malley questioned, "How was Mortimer's information related to you?"

Bill recognized that his prior chief inspector was in his element. He answered, "That is an excellent question. I have examined it many times. It was one of the few written communications that I received from him during this entire operation. It was concise and encoded. It definitely was relating to me his concern about a leak in his operation. It did not specifically point to our side of the operation. That was an interpretation that was drawn from our first analysis. It could have just as equally been construed as being a member of his own chosen local team."

"That's an important finding," admitted O'Malley. "Detective Joe Barrett is beginning to collect evidence that may support this theory. In addition, Mr. Anthony Willard is vigorously pursuing this avenue with his own resources."

Bill Normandin added, "What Joe Barrett reported about Mortimer's creative way of concealing the cash for his operation on his person speaks to his flair for the unusual and the even bizarre activities of his youth. This was an unexpected and important discovery by Joe. By the way, how is he? The last time we met you mentioned that he was not feeling well and was planning to retire."

O'Malley informed Bill, "Joe struggles with his asthma during these hot and humid days. The Chief has accepted his plan to retire on the last day of September. He will be moving to upstate New York to live with his daughter and family. He'll be missed. He was an excellent detective and a good team player. His one ambition is to solve the mystery of Mortimer Weigand before he leaves the force."

Bill asked, "Are you planning a farewell event? I would like to be part of it. I learned an awful lot from him especially in my early years as a rookie cop. He would slip me a clue or suggest an approach. He never wanted to claim the success of solving a case solely for himself. It was always a team victory."

O'Malley told Bill, "We are planning something for the last Saturday of the month. That's only a few weeks away. When the details are finalized, I will pass on the information. We haven't had a good party since the Chief retired."

Two by Each
Chapter Forty-nine

Russ Oliver was again in Mr. Willard's office presenting his latest information. "This past week I hung around the croquet club on a week day. My past visit had been on a Saturday. I met a different group of members than the ones who frequented the place on the weekend. They'd heard of my visit and I began to learn that they assumed that I was from the neighborhood and probably checking if I wanted to become a member. That provided a different atmosphere. The men were pleasant and more forthcoming."

"That's good," commented Mr. Willard. "What did you learn?" The bank president was preoccupied with other matters and expressed his impatience.

Russ continued his report, "Most importantly I learned that at about the time that you released Claude from his service at Mortimer's residence, he began to hang out there during the day. It was only on Monday or Tuesday since he was very busy at his restaurant for the remainder of the week. He again played a lot of croquet, even winning a trophy. In the afternoons he played cards. Most members volunteered that he ran into a streak of bad luck. The wagers on these games are small and no one indicated that Claude owed anyone money. Those small amounts, however, do add up after a while and they said that he had stopped frequenting the club about two weeks ago."

Mr. Willard while reflecting on his own experience ventured an opinion, "As you mentioned, gambling losses do accumulate. Where were these funds coming from? His restaurant business slows down in the summer months. With his loan and other expenses, I don't expect that he had a lot of extra cash available to support his gambling habit."

Later that afternoon Inspector O'Malley visited the bank president's office at his invitation. Mr. Willard had indicated over the telephone that he had some further information to share with him.

After offering O'Malley a chair in front of his desk, Mr. Willard reported, "My sources indicate that the men who worked with Mortimer seemed clean. There was one unexpected exception and that was his chauffeur, Claude Lepage. He liked to play at cards and most likely beyond his financial limits. We know that Claude participated in the cash transactions for Mortimer's operation. He actually handled the manila envelopes filled with cash at the post office. He also dropped off the payments in the wrapped up newspaper. He reported to your detective that he didn't know the contents of these packages. Could he have become curious and discovered what was inside them? Would he have been tempted to help himself to some of it?"

O'Malley remarked, "We can investigate that matter. If anyone was short in their payments, it could have presented a major difficulty for Mortimer. The men on the docks play hardball. I'll have my team look into this avenue."

"Also for your information," Mr. Willard continued, "I learned that Claude secured his loan with a new bank in town with a cash deposit of $350.00. That's a lot of cash for someone in his financial status. I don't have any proof and now have a lot of suspicions about Claude Lepage. Maybe you can pull something together. If I come across any other details of interest, I'll inform you. My sources are still pursuing the disappearance of Mortimer for me."

Two by Each
Chapter Fifty

Detective Joe Barrett welcomed this new piece of information. "These circumstances certainly give my investigation a whole different direction. I only have two more weeks to wrap this up."

O'Malley appreciated his detective's commitment and integrity to the process of investigating this very unusual event.

O'Malley started, "I'm having difficulty applying a label to the case. Is it a homicide? Certainly Mortimer Weigand has not been seen or heard from for almost a year now. Or is it a case of a missing person? Was that intentional on Mortimer's part? Or is it a robbery that precipitated the whole affair?"

Joe Barrett asked, "Can you assign my other cases to someone else? I would like to pursue this new line of investigation about Claude's possible involvement. There are a number of people that I would like to question."

O'Malley readily agreed, "I'll inform the other detectives of this abrupt change. Just help in transferring your files to the persons on your team. We needed to start doing that anyhow. Who are some of the people you hope to interrogate?"

Joe answered, "First, I'd like to question Carlos Frias, the owner of the shop that installed the navigation systems. I want to find out and interrogate all the fishing industry people who were referred to him by Mortimer, including Arthur Lerner the owner of the Puffin. He's the only one I've spoken to so far and I've discovered how crude and tough these fishing and dock workers can be. Second, I want to investigate the opening of Claude's fish and chip establishment. I'd like to talk with the previous owner and any of the staff, especially those who may have stayed on. I plan to officially review the details of the loan referred to by Mr. Willard and trace the origin of the down payment. Third, dependent on what I discover, I believe Claude himself needs to be cross-examined by the both of us. He's beginning to look like a person of interest."

"That sounds like a plan," said O'Malley. "Any time you need my assistance, just give a shout. You'll be one of my priorities."

Two by Each
Chapter Fifty-one

The following Tuesday morning Joe Barrett was having one of his final meetings with the inspector. Joe looked exhausted.

O'Malley cautioned, "Don't let this case get to you. We've had our share of cases where the evidence we collected wasn't good enough for the prosecutor's office."

Joe answered, "I appreciate what you are saying. However, somehow I've taken this one on as my final act prior to my going to the green fields of New York. I've asked myself the question, How did I let this get under my skin? Maybe it's affirming that it's time for me to retire."

O'Malley questioned, "How were your interviews?"

"First," answered Joe, "Carlos Frias provided me with five names. All are small fishing boat owners. Only Arthur Lerner owns more than one boat and he captains both of them. Of the others, one is from Norway, two are Portuguese – one from the mainland of Portugal and the other from the Islands. Even though they speak the same language, they both emphasize the differences in their background. However, the two of them were both similar in being very reticent and cautious despite their emphasis on being unique. The other one was originally from England."

Joe continued, "The boat owners from Norway and England were very congenial and easy-going. Both loved to share their stories with me. The one from Norway came here prior to the Nazi occupation of his country. What he told me about his family's life in Norway during the occupation was quite unbelievable. The old news reels of the war we saw in the movie theaters came back to me. However, these were real people to him and not just someone in a film. The guy from England was funny. He supposedly travelled the world as an attaché for the Crown – as he called it. He converted a shrimp boat into a dragger so that he could fish off these northern shores. He named his boat the Millpoint. None of these four men projected any sense of discord with Mr. Mortimer Weigand. They appreciated receiving the new radio equipment. No one has further contacted them after Mortimer's disappearance."

"Arthur Lerner is a different sort all together. As you know he's uncouth, self-absorbed and not so much respected but feared by his crews. Other fishermen all know him and keep a safe distance. From your report and my two interviews, I don't see him as a suspect. He seemingly liked Mortimer and I doubt if greed would have elicited such an act. He's rude and vulgar but has no history of being a violent man."

O'Malley added, "Bill Normandin supports your discovery that these fishermen were dropped from the FBI operation. He told me that Mortimer's operation was shut down shortly after his disappearance. However, we know by solid police work that we were able to discover those men. Bill Normandin and his superiors didn't want to bring any attention to the FBI and any other parts of the clandestine operation that is still operational."

Joe Barrett scratched his head, "One thing that I can't get my head around. It's the time that elapsed between when Arthur Lerner dropped off Mortimer at his office on Sunday night and Claude's alleged discovery of his body on Monday morning. Nothing in his office was seemingly out of place, his files were not rifled, and there were no signs of a break-in or altercation." Joe Barrett continued, "I have had a little more success in my investigation of Claude's bank loan. I was able to track down the accountant who had assisted in the sale of the restaurant. His wife who acts as his secretary and bookkeeper readily informed me that Claude's in-laws, the Saulniers, had provided $250.00 for a down payment. When I informed her that my sources had indicated that the amount of the down payment was $350.00, she looked perplexed and couldn't provide any answer to the discrepancy."

The inspector informed Joe Barrett, "I've contacted Mr. Willard at the bank and basically he couldn't add any additional information to what he had already shared with me. I think it's time to pick up Claude Lepage. I'll set it for eight o'clock tomorrow morning."

Two by Each
Chapter Fifty-two

So on a Wednesday morning in September almost ten months after Claude's discovery of Mortimer Weigand's body, Claude was sitting in the downtown police station. He was in the sterile interview room sitting at a table with Inspector O'Malley across from him and Detective Joe Barrett standing to the side in view of both of them, as was his custom.

Claude was evidently quite shaken. The color on his face was ashen. The two policemen in the room could hear the nervous twitching and jumping of Claude's leg under the interview table. He had not anticipated another interrogation session.

The inspector started, "Claude, you are aware that the disappearance of your prior employer has not been solved. However, new information suggested that we probe more deeply into your role in this mystery. Recently we've discovered some troubling aspects about you that might put in jeopardy the truthfulness of your past statements. Up to now we have had no reason not to take your statements at face value."

Detective Barrett approached the table and looking down at Claude bluntly stated, "We have learned that you are a habitual card player and that you have had what you call a streak of bad luck. What do you have to say about this?"

Claude was now physically shaking all over. He turned down his eyes from looking at the Detective, and then glanced at the always courteous inspector looking for some reassurance. O'Malley spoke softly but firmly, "Just answer the Detective's question."

Claude was confused. He wasn't sure how the police had discovered this about him. He only played cards at the croquet club which he had thought was a great cover. Someone must have squealed on him. Someone who had been jealous of the overconfident attitude he had exhibited during his long winning streak had turned on him now that he was losing.

O'Malley reiterated his statement, "Please answer the Detective's question."

"Let's break it down and make this easier," said Barrett. "Do you play cards?

"Yes," answered Claude.

"Good," stated Barrett. "Now that wasn't so difficult, was it?"

Claude nodded his head.

Barrett continued, "Do you gamble money when you play cards?"

Again Claude hesitated. Money was never on the card tables. The croquet club had designed a concealed method of wagering. He didn't want to get them in trouble.

O'Malley interrupted Claude's ponderings.

"Claude, this is a yes or no question. Please answer the Detective."

"Yes," admitted Claude.

"Thank you," answered Barrett. "Have you been on a losing streak?"

Claude hesitated briefly, "Yes." Then he added, "but I've stopped gambling."

O'Malley said, "We were informed of that."

Joe Barrett continued the interrogation, "Are you in any debt?"

Claude was finding this cross-examination difficult. He said truthfully, "I do not owe any money to the members of the club."

"How did you manage to do that?" continued Joe.

Claude answered quickly, "My wife and I have money set aside from the fish and chip store to help us during the slower summer season. I used that money to pay for my losses."

The Detective continued, "Did the drawing down of that money from your savings present any difficulties?"

Claude realized suddenly that he had put himself into a corner. Only his brother Al had recently been made aware of this situation. Even his wife Anne was still in the dark. A few times after he had told Al of his problem he had tried to tell Anne but he would lose his nerve.

O'Malley encouraged Claude, "What is your present financial situation?"

"We're in a bit of a hole," Claude answered. "But one of my brothers is helping us out."

Joe Barrett cut in, "How much of a hole are you in? And with whom?"

Claude recognized that this was getting tough and answered, "I was able to get a week's credit with my fish distributor. That credit needs to be paid before they will release another weekly order of fish. Our savings won't cover what we owe. My brother Al is in a position to make up the difference for this week. However, the order of fish for the current week is larger since business is picking up now that schools have reopened."

"So you are in a bit of a jam," exclaimed Barrett.

Claude acknowledged with a nod.

O'Malley abruptly changed the subject, "How did you manage to finance the purchase of your new restaurant?"

Claude experienced a sigh of relief. This line of questioning would be easier. "We got a loan from a bank on Coffin Avenue."

Barrett jumped in, "How did you manage that?"

Claude answered, "The former owner's accountant helped us with the paper work and my wife Anne's parents gave us a down payment."

"How much was the down payment with the bank?" Barrett continued.

"We put down $350.00," said Claude.

"Is that the amount Anne's parents gave you?" inquired Barrett.

Claude hesitated. This was getting tricky again. The police seemed to know a lot more about this situation than he had thought.

"It's a simple question," insisted the detective.

"No, it isn't," answered Claude. He added, "The Saulniers gave us $250.00 from their savings and I put in the extra $100.00."

"Where did you get that extra $100.00?" asked Barrett.

Claude wondered to himself, how much of this do they know? The only person who knew anything about his secret stash was his former boss, Mr. Weigand, and certainly he hadn't been talking.

Again O'Malley encouraged, "Please explain this matter to us."

"It's a long story," started Claude. "For over a year during my work as Mr. Weigand's chauffeur, he would give me ten dollars for running extra errands for him. That was my play money. I used those funds to meet the requirements of obtaining the loan."

"So you and Mr. Weigand had some arrangements that were not part of your regular duties," stated Barrett. "What was the nature of those errands?"

Claude answered quickly, "I have already told that to you. Mr. Weigand would have me deliver a folded newspaper at various places in the city."

O'Malley commented, "In your past statement on this subject, you told us that you had no idea what that delivery meant or contained. You assumed that it was some bit of information for one of Mr. Weigand's contacts. You also stated that the few people whom you observed picking up the paper parcels were not Mr. Weigand's professional contacts, but dock workers or fishermen. Do you still agree with my version of your previous statement?"

"Yes," agreed Claude.

Barrett again jumped in, "Did your curiosity ever get you to look into the folded newspaper?"

Claude again faltered.

O'Malley urged Claude, "Please answer the Detective."

Reluctantly Claude spoke, "I think it is best that I start all over again."

Two by Each
Chapter Fifty-three

As Inspector O'Malley eased back into his chair he thought, they were finally getting somewhere. Detective Joe Barrett continued to stare down on Claude. He wasn't about to let up on the last interrogation of his long career.

"Where do I start?" questioned Claude.

O'Malley said, "I suggest you start at the beginning."

Joe Barret added, "Just give us the facts not the story."

Claude started, "Some months before I found Mr. Weigand in his office, I became suspicious of some of his activities. The manila envelopes that I picked up at the post office suggested to me that they could possibly be money. As I felt the package the contents felt the right size and weight. This I would give over immediately to Mr. Weigand when I returned to the car. So I never had the chance to check them out"

Claude looked up to the detective who encouraged him to go on. "I soon put together that my deliveries of the folded newspapers and the manila envelopes were related. Mr. Weigand would leave the folded newspaper on the back seat of the car. He would give me verbal directions as to where to drop the newsprint. It was standard that the delivery time was at noon. One day my curiosity got the better of me. I unfolded the paper and found an envelope and even with it sealed I knew for sure that it contained paper money."

Joe Barrett asked, "Did you take some of that money?"

"I did once but I put the money back," answered Claude.

225

O'Malley questioned, "Did Mortimer Weigand ever suspect that you did this?"

"Yes," answered Claude. "One time I took a one hundred dollar bill out of the envelope. On the next delivery I replaced that amount in the envelope. The hundred had covered my losses until my luck started going in the right direction. A few days later as I brought some items to his office on Center Street, he asked me to close the door of the office. This was very unusual. I became anxious but tried to keep my calm."

"What did Mr. Weigand have to say?" quizzed Joe Barrett.

"He pointedly asked me if I had taken any money from any of my prior deliveries. He was so direct that I confessed to the act but added immediately that I had returned the money in the next delivery," answered Claude.

He continued, "Rigidness took over his facial expression and he screeched, 'You fool!' and then added, 'You've put my whole operation in jeopardy.' Then he continued, 'Did you think that every delivery went to the same person?' It suddenly struck me what I had done. The first recipient had been shorted a hundred dollars."

Claude continued, "Mr. Weigand gained control and added, 'I was made aware of the shortage and the person wasn't happy. He thought he could trust me and my deal with him. I'm not sure I can regain that trust. In addition his account of the incident is spreading.' He was livid. He told me that he was completely blindsided by my action as he had trusted me. Now he wasn't sure how to proceed."

Claude continued, "The next few weeks were strained and nerve-wracking. Mr. Weigand was evidently very agitated and short-tempered with me. Then that Monday morning I found him hanging in his office."

Joe Barrett bent over the side of the table and firmly questioned, "Are these the facts or just another story?" Claude was frightened and again looked to the inspector for reassurance.

O'Malley calmly asked Claude "Is there anything you wish add or subtract from the description of that incident?"

"No," answered Claude. "I described what I came upon in that office that morning."

Joe Barrett insisted, "Is there anything about this incident that you're not telling us?"

Claude breathed in deeply and closing his eyes for a moment finally said, "Mr. Weigand had me over a barrel. He forced me into being part of a plan to disappear from sight. Everything was staged. He feared that some secret plan that he was part of was unravelling and that his life was a total failure and embarrassment."

O'Malley inquired, "Did Mortimer Weigand explain the nature of this secret operation?"

Claude answered, "All he said is that it was government related and highly secretive. He called on my military training and commitment to the nation to assist him in not only disappearing from sight but that he had come to a tragic death. I thought the plan was quite over the edge. He had me assist him in developing a noose that would go around his shoulders and that would hold him off the ground. We also provided a light string that was attached to his tied up hands. With the string he was able to pull the heavy cord from the peg on the wall that would drop him to the ground after I left the room. However, he insisted that I view the scene so that I would be able to describe it in detail. He came up with the blackened tongue and soiled trouser so as to add reality to the scene. It was gruesome. It actually made me sick."

O'Malley asked further, "What were his plans following this staging of his hanging?"

"He didn't tell me," answered Claude. "I don't think he could trust me. There was only one thing he asked me to do for him. He asked me to mail a letter he had written to my sister and to wait a few days before doing so. He wanted to give her a message that he was okay. He didn't want to leave any traces."

"So it's your supposition that Mortimer Weigand is alive and in hiding," concluded Joe Barrett.

"I think that was his plan," answered Claude.

O'Malley asked, "Did he give you any indication as to how he would support himself?"

Claude answered, "As Mr. Weigand's plan was developing, we travelled to Newport, Rhode Island. He met with an old friend from his days in the Naval Academy. This friend may know where Mr. Weigand is and may be helping him. That's my best guess."

Two by Each
Chapter Fifty-four

The retirement party for Detective Joe Barrett was held at a neighborhood bar on Acushnet Avenue not far from the struggling New Bedford Hotel. It was a favorite hangout for downtown city officials after long hours of work and meetings.

It was a relatively small group. Joe Barrett had made many friends over the years but he had been a rather quiet guy and did not frequent watering holes after a day's work, especially during his wife's illness and after her death. He was well liked and most had congratulated him personally prior to his retirement. That fit much better with his style and temperament. He appreciated the individual conversations rather than the raucous banter and retelling of stories that was so often the part of a group gathering over a few beers.

The party hadn't lasted too long. Chief Luke Guerney was in attendance and presented Joe with a gift from the department. Inspector O'Malley had to silence the group so that the chief could make his presentation. The chief started, "Joe, the members of the department after much deliberation have decided to gift you with something that will come in handy as you go into retirement in the vast farmlands of upstate New York." He opened an unwrapped box and pulled out for all to see a set of gray coveralls. The group cheered and well wishes echoed in the room – referencing milking cows, shoveling manure and plowing fields.

The group gradually broke up. It was a Saturday night and most had families waiting for them. Contrary to his normal practice, Joe Barrett stayed on to the very end – after all he was the guest of honor. Two people had remained behind with Joe, Inspector O'Malley and FBI Agent Bill Normandin.

Bill drew Joe and O'Malley aside to a quiet corner in the bar. Bill said, "I wanted to bring you up to date on the Mortimer case. We were easily able to locate his Naval Academy friend whose family still lives in Newport. He was able to assure us that Mortimer was fine. Other details you don't need to know. The Bureau has decided to maintain his cover and not pursue it further. They are asking your local police department to put the case on file. My superiors have already contacted your chief and the city mayor. Joe, congratulations. You solved the mystery before going into retirement."

ABOUT THE AUTHOR

Clement R. Beaulieu is a semi-retired income tax preparer. In the off-season he recently wrote and published two historical mystery novels entitled, *Bad Lucky Number*, circa 1930, and *Round Corners*, circa 1940, set in the mill city of New Bedford, MA. He lives with his wife, Jo-Ann in the quaint neighboring town of Fairhaven. They have two daughters, Sarah and Julia, who live nearby.

Contact the author at:
Clement R. Beaulieu
346 Sconticut Neck Road
Fairhaven, MA 02719-1318
Phone: 508-993-8659
CLEMCTP@COMCAST.NET